SHROUDED GLORY

A WWII NOVEL

CHRIS GLATTE

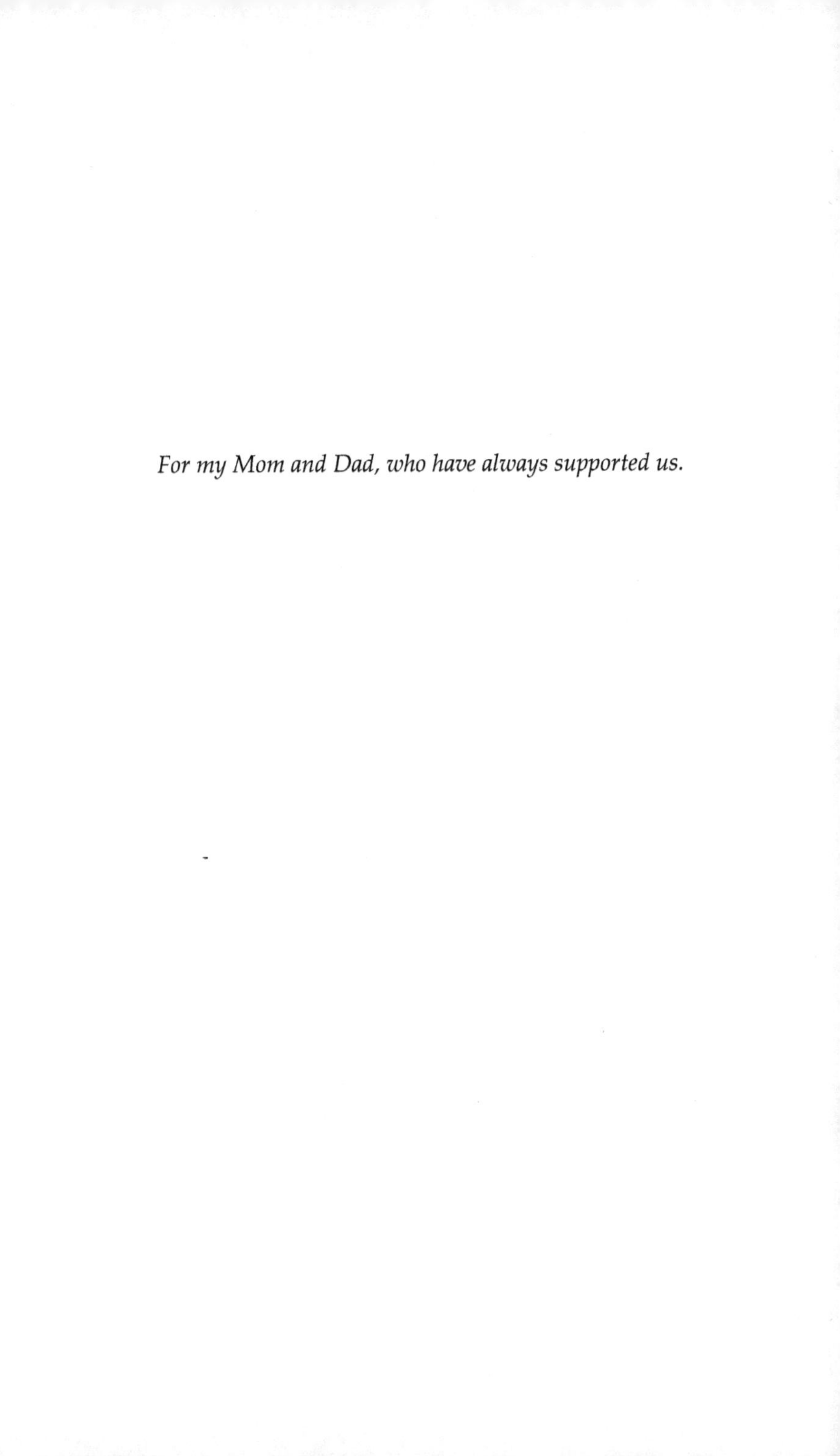

For my Mom and Dad, who have always supported us.

1

Private Mankowitz shivered as he stood on the deck of the troop transport ship. Other soldiers surrounded him from the 32nd Regiment of the 7th Infantry Division. Despite the cold, he was glad to be getting off the ship.

The soldier beside him, Private Harwick, elbowed Mankowitz. "This is it. They won't call it off this time around."

Mankowitz nodded. "Finally. I'd rather face the Japs than spend another miserable night below decks."

Harwick smiled, showing off crooked teeth. "Me too." His pinched face turned serious, "Think they're waiting for us on the beach?"

Mankowitz shrugged, "Fog's so thick I can barely see the shore from here. If they could see us, they'd be shelling the boats by now, I guess."

"Yeah, guess you're right. Hope the fog doesn't lift or we'll be sitting ducks."

"I'm just glad we're finally loading. We've been standing here freezing our asses off for..." he checked his wristwatch, "six hours now." He wondered how long the wristwatch would last in the wet conditions.

Harwick nodded, "At least we got some hot soup."

Mankowitz blew warm breath into his gloved hands. The gloves weren't army issue; they—along with a scarf, were a gift from his mother. He'd laughed, reminding her he was on his way to the baking California desert for training and wouldn't have much use for them. She insisted, though, and now that he was in the icy north, he was thankful.

Because they'd trained in desert conditions, everyone assumed they'd be sent to North Africa to fight the Germans. However, now they were anchored off Attu Island, the western-most island in the Alaskan Aleutian chain, to fight Japanese. The island, or at least the surrounding sea, was wet and cold. Mankowitz doubted all the months of training and acclimatizing to the desert environment would translate too well. He hadn't been in the US Army long, but long enough to know they didn't always operate on logic.

The guns from Task Force 51's destroyers and cruisers opened fire. The shells arced over their heads and disappeared into the fog. The crumps of exploding ordinance sounded muffled, and he couldn't see the explosions at all. He wondered how they knew what they were shooting at.

Captain Smith barked, "Okay, men. Over the side. Let's get this done."

Mankowitz and Harwick exchanged glances and checked one another's gear. "See you on the boat, Mank," called Harwick.

Private Mankowitz's mouth was suddenly dry as desert sand and he couldn't reply. He nodded instead and took a step toward the rope netting hanging over the side of the transport. Soldiers in front stepped over the side carefully and disappeared. Some gave quick, nervous glances to the men still waiting.

Mankowitz's thoughts went to his best friend from high school, Mack Hunter. He desperately wished he was by his side now, but he'd gotten a wild hair up his ass and volunteered for the newly formed Provisional Battalion. Though their purpose was a mystery, it required more training and had a high drop-out rate.

The mystique and commando-style training was too much for his naturally gifted best friend to resist. He'd begged him to join too, but he had no desire for that sort of thing. Before parting for his special training, they'd both taken part in an amphibious landing exercise put on by the legendary Marine General 'Howlin' Mad' Smith. Afterwards, they'd shaken hands, and parted ways. He hadn't seen his friend since.

He got a letter a few weeks later. Mack had made it through the tough training and joined the 7th Scout Company. As they sailed from San Francisco, Mankowitz heard the unit was in the convoy but on a different troop ship and was heading in the same direction—north. He'd heard rumors that the Scout Company would land at a separate beach somewhere east of Holz Bay and would eventually link up with the 32nd Regiment. He looked forward to that day. It comforted him knowing his friend would chew some of the same ground.

It was Mankowitz's turn to go over the side. He gazed down. The net reminded him of a massive spider's web, full of struggling prey. The Higgins Boat, rocking below, was taking on the first soldiers. It looked small from up here, but he knew it could easily carry three squads of GIs. He swung his legs over and found the horizontal ropes. He descended slowly, reminding himself to only grasp the vertical ropes or risk getting his hand stepped on by the soldier above.

The weight of his pack threatened to pull him from the net, but he held fast and moved efficiently. He finally stepped from the net and onto the Higgins' hard deck. Sergeant Calder was there, pushing him forward, "Move it along. Come on, let's go. We don't got all day, ladies."

Mankowitz pushed forward and soon felt the man behind pressed up against his back. They were packed in tight.

Mankowitz closed his eyes, staving off the claustrophobic feeling creeping over him.

The idling engines revved, and the Higgins Boat turned away from the transport and motored into the calm waters of Massacre Bay. Mankowitz chanced a look over the side. The fog had lifted a little and he could see the black shale on the beach. Snow-covered, stark mountains surrounded the sloping valley. Fog shrouded the tops, but the steep slopes leading up to them looked treacherous and besides the snow, featureless.

He'd gotten glimpses of the peaks from the transport ship. As far as he could tell, there wasn't a tree growing on the entire island. Native Alaskan scouts told them the ground was covered with a thin layer of tundra. They warned them about treacherous holes and crevices filled with bottomless mud.

The Higgin's driver turned in lazy circles awaiting the rest of the landing force to join. The naval artillery continued, although the intensity had died down, and Mankowitz figured it was because there'd been no return fire. The Japanese had taken the island a year before and were used to getting bombed and shelled. They probably thought this was more of the same. If there were enemy troops on the beach, they'd have to be blind not to see them, but so far there'd been no hostile fire.

Finally, the driver yelled through a bullhorn, "Hold onto your asses! We're going in." The throb of the 225-horsepower diesel engine increased and soon they were chugging toward the beach at 12 knots. Sea spray drifted over them, but the adrenaline coursing through Mankowitz's blood stream made him forget about the cold. Harwick was to his left. He was shorter than Mankowitz and he had his head down, staring at his boots.

Mankowitz found his voice. "Here we go. Holy shit! It's really happening."

Harwick looked up at him and grinned. Mankowitz thought his face was paler than normal, but that might just be the cold. Harwick's gaze went back to the deck and Mankowitz mulled over for the thousandth time what the officers and NCOs had been telling them for weeks. When the door opens, move up as far as possible to clear the way for the next wave. That was it. It was an easy, uncomplicated assignment. That didn't keep the doubt and fear from creeping in though. What if the Japs had a machine gun nest directly in front of them? What if the Japs charged them? What if they mined the beach? He shook his head. It was no use worrying, whatever was going to happen couldn't be helped now.

The Navy coxswain yelled, "One minute."

The dual .30 caliber machine guns mounted on either side of the boat were silent, which made him feel better. If there were enemy troops visible, they'd be firing by now. He wasn't a religious man, at least not any more than the next man. He considered sending up a prayer but thought it might come as a surprise to whoever was up there listening, so he didn't.

The engine cut to idle and the boat mushed into the sea, then abruptly slid onto the rocky beach. The loud squeak of the front hatch dropping, followed immediately by it slamming into the ankle-deep water, made Mankowitz jolt back to the present. How the hell had he been daydreaming? Someone yelled, "Go! Go! Go!"

Mankowitz lurched from the boat and splashed into the water. His high laced leather boots dug into the shale and he sprinted after the soldier in front of him. He recognized Private Lance, the squad's grenadier. He expected to be shot at any moment, but there was nothing but the wind and fog.

Private Lance ran until the beach turned to grass, then threw himself against the lip it formed. He brought his M1 Garand to his shoulder as Mankowitz rolled in beside him. Between breaths, Mankowitz sputtered, "See anything?"

More men slid in beside them and soon the entire squad was there. Lance lowered his head from the lip and shook it. "Nah. Nothing but grass and fog."

Harwick took his pack off. He was barely breathing hard, but his eyes were wide, filling most of his scrunched face. "Think they saw us coming and left?"

Lance shook his head. "Hell, if they saw you coming, they'd be invading Seattle by now."

Harwick scowled at him. "What the hell's that supposed to mean?"

Lance's grin widened, "Cause one look at you and they'd think they were fighting children."

Harwick's eyes went to slits. His temper was legendary. Despite his small stature, he wasn't afraid to fight, and since he'd been dealing with people making fun of his size his entire life, he was damned good at it.

Sergeant Calder intervened, "Knock it off. First squad, we're moving up to that cover." He pointed to a mound covered in bent dead grass thirty yards ahead. "Move out, Team One! We'll cover you."

Mankowitz got to his feet and took off, keeping his profile as low as possible. He'd dumped his heavy pack and didn't feel as though he were running through taffy anymore. The other five GIs were to either side, keeping a ten-yard interval. They got to the little knoll at the same instant and went into crouches, their M1s at the ready. The land in all directions was empty of anything living.

The rest of the squad moved up and joined them. Soon the rest of Second Platoon moved inland, bringing First Squad's packs to them.

The fog continued to waft in and out, sometimes cutting visibility to twenty yards. The black shale rock gave way to tundra. It felt spongy. Mankowitz had never felt anything like it. He commented to Harwick, "Feels like we're walking on an angel food cake my mom baked."

Harwick cursed, "Dammit, Mank. Stop talking about food. I'm hungry enough already."

After moving one hundred yards up the valley, Lieutenant Hubert called a halt. They still hadn't seen anything other than a few ravens. The wind whipped up and Mankowitz shivered and pulled the collar of his wool coat tighter around his neck, but the wind cut straight through and he shivered. He silently thanked his mother for giving him the scarf.

A few minutes later, Sergeant Jakant barked, "We're digging in until the rest of the Company joins us. Don't get too comfortable, should be here pretty damned quick."

Mankowitz pulled his trusty entrenching tool. It was scratched and worn down from scraping and cutting through the dense California desert. He relished the soft ground of Attu. "This'll be a piece of cake," he muttered to Harwick. He jabbed it into the soft ground and scooped large chunks of grass and tundra. He was almost giddy until he got about two feet down. His blade sunk into a morass of black, oily mud. It was the consistency of thick soup and had a smell he couldn't quite place. A cross between a dead animal and burnt oil. It flowed as though there was a river of mud just beneath the tundra grasses.

Harwick reared back, "Damn, that stinks. We gotta lay in that?"

Mankowitz kept scraping the black mud from the hole until he finally got to something solid. It sounded and felt like rock, but upon further inspection, he realized it was frozen ground. He sighed, "I'm not sure I'm gonna like this place after all."

Harwick nodded his agreement then shrugged, "At least there ain't any Japs."

Private Mack Hunter shivered as the wind cut through his heavy wool clothes and whipped icy sea spray into his face. The submarine USS Narwohl gently submerged beneath their black rubber boat, leaving them and six other boats, floating. Lieutenant Wilcox waited a few seconds until the submarine's mast was completely out of sight, then signaled them to paddle.

Private Hunter was happy to comply. The movement would help keep him warm. It was the middle of the night and pitch black. He took up a steady cadence along with the other men of 3rd Squad from 3rd Platoon. The rubber boat plowed through the water quietly. Lieutenant Wilcox corrected their angle from the stern as he watched his wrist mounted compass.

Hunter's sharp eyes picked out the outlines of mountains. Large patches of snow showed up even in the darkest of nights and he could see their little armada of rubber boats was entering a small bay surrounded by low hills and steep mountains. He knew from the briefing that they were paddling through the waters of Austin Cove. He didn't know where it had gotten its name, but he thought it was close enough to austere, to fit.

His gloved hands went through painful pins and needles as the numbness wore off. Finally, the boat kissed the beach. He stowed his paddle between the thwarts and the floor, pulled his M1 carbine off his shoulder, and watched the four GIs in the bow hustle into the darkness. No one expected the beach to be defended, but there was only one way to find out.

A few tense minutes passed. More boats touched the beach. The rest of the 7th Scout Company coming off the second submarine, Nautilus, had arrived.

There was no firing, although he wasn't sure he'd be able to hear much over the whistling, biting wind. He saw no muzzle flashes and nothing that looked like enemy movement.

Finally, his squad members returned and gave Lieutenant Wilcox the all clear. He signaled and Hunter and the others offloaded packs and gear. They hefted the mostly empty boats up the beach and hid them as best they could in a ravine.

Even through the exertion, Hunter wasn't warm. They had issued the Provisional Battalion cold weather gear, but he still felt underdressed. He wondered what his best friend John Mankowitz was doing at that exact moment. Probably warm and sleeping comfortably in the hull of some rust bucket transport ship off Massacre Bay. The thought made him colder. It was times like these, he wished he'd stayed with his buddy from Charlie Company.

They signaled the submarines loitering off the cove that they'd landed successfully. There was no responding light signal the enemy might spot. Their mission was underway, and so far, they were on schedule.

Lieutenant Wilcox muttered an order to Staff Sergeant Rizzo and soon 3rd Platoon was leading the company along the little creek bisecting the valley which drained the looming mountains beyond.

Hunter had viewed the terrain, first from the escorting destroyer's deck, then again from the mast of the submarine a few days later. The mountains were beautiful but constantly enshrouded in fog, rain, and spitting-wet snow. He'd grown up in the forests and mountains of Montana, hunting and fishing with his two brothers and best friend John. This tree-less land was like something he imagined on the moon. Despite the cold and the occupying Japanese, he couldn't keep the excitement of exploration off his mind. The Alaskan scouts who'd briefed them, said there wasn't much wildlife to speak of, a few imported foxes. This place was as wild as they came though, and he couldn't wait to learn its hidden secrets.

2

———

Private Mack Hunter was on point, leading the long string of men up the mountains separating Austin Cove from the west arm of Holz Bay. He hadn't seen the enemy, or even any sign that they'd ever been there. The darkness combined with freezing rain and thick layers of fog didn't help matters. At first, he'd worried he might lead them into an ambush, but the further he trudged, the more convinced he became that there wasn't another human being within miles.

The snow deepened as they gained elevation. Icy wind hit him in the face, and he wondered how the fog managed to hang on. It was as though it wasn't air, but something solid. His mind wandered and he imagined it wasn't fog at all, but some massive, angry spirit.

Breaking trail through the knee-deep, heavy snow was exhausting. He was in the best shape of his life, but his pace slowed, and he was thankful to rotate his position.

A few hours later, they crested a tall peak and halted for the night. There wasn't much cover from the incessant wind. They dug themselves into the snow and laid upon their thin ponchos. The cold seeped into their bones and Hunter wished they'd been issued sleeping bags. They were considered too bulky and heavy for the long march up the mountains. They would be airdropped to them, along with more food and ammunition once it was light enough to see. For now, all they could do was huddle together and shiver.

Daylight finally came. Hunter was astonished that he'd slept a little. There was a thick layer of fog below them. Tendrils swirled around the peak, and the sky was overcast, but it was the clearest he'd seen the island so far. He hoped the supply plane would find them. He didn't relish spending another night out here without a sleeping bag and his K-rations were already depleted by half. The constant strain of keeping warm and struggling up mountains through deep snow gave them all quite an appetite. Without the supply drop, they'd be in deep trouble.

They carried two day's worth of food. Their mission was to hit the enemy garrison in Holz Bay quickly, keeping them occupied and away from the main force landing further north on Red Beach. The planners figured taking Attu from the Japanese wouldn't take more than three days, so keeping the 7th Scout Company light was paramount to their successful mission. They expected to meet up with the rest of the 32nd and 17th Regiments no later than tomorrow.

Captain Willoughby came from the hole he'd spent the night in and stretched his back. Hunter crouched nearby, watching the wispy fog to the east. Lieutenant Wilcox, his platoon leader, was talking. "We're on the correct mountain top, sir." He pointed east, "Holz Bay is four miles that way. Once we get resupplied, we can move out."

Willoughby nodded and blew warm air into his hands and stomped his feet. "Could've used a sleeping bag last night." The look on Wilcox's face was, "No shit," but he only nodded. Willoughby continued. "Our 284s and 195 radios are giving us fits, but we've contacted the 11th flyboys. They're on their way." He looked up, "They shouldn't have any trouble finding us today. Get ready to fire flares in case they need some help." He pointed, "Send a squad forward. Find us the best route to the bay."

"Yes, sir."

Willoughby strolled off to take a piss, and Lieutenant Wilcox relayed the orders to Staff Sergeant Rizzo. "Get your men fed and find the best route to the valley. We'll wait here for the drop. Send someone back to guide us and we'll join you soon enough."

Rizzo noticed Hunter and Private Gentry listening in and barked, "You get all that?" He shook his head. "Get some food before you go." His hard eyes drilled into Hunter's. "You're on point again."

Hunter got to his feet and nodded, "Yes, Sergeant." Rizzo found his assistant squad leader and gave him the scoop.

Private Gentry crouched beside Hunter. He growled, "Hell-fire—we the only platoon on this mountaintop?"

Hunter slapped him on the back, "The Captain just knows who he can rely on, that's all."

"Shit. You're blowing smoke up my ass, Mack." He looked at the shifting cloud cover overhead, "I'm down to my last K-rat. Hope the flyboys find us soon."

Hunter shook his head. "I don't know how they can even find the island, let alone this peak. Hope they know what they're doing or we're in for a hard time."

Gentry slurped in cold chunks of meat. "Just gotta get through today, then we'll hook up with the 32nd and we won't need the airdrops anymore." He grinned, "Hell, Japs might've already left. I sure the hell wouldn't wanna stick around this miserable place for long."

Hunter stopped opening his can and looked out over the vastness. "Beautiful out here if you can get past the cold and wet."

Gentry shook his head, "There's a reason no one lives out here, you know. Hell, there aren't even any animals to hunt. You'd die of boredom if you didn't freeze to death first."

Hunter continued working the lid off the can. "People live here. Not many, but those Alaskan Scouts said there's a tiny village up Chichagof Valley. Fifty people or so."

"Miserable life," Gentry mumbled.

JUST BEFORE DARKNESS fell on Massacre Bay, the roar of three 105mm Howitzers reverberated through the fog. Two more salvos, then silence. The low crumps from their impacts seemed to be absorbed by the fog and looming darkness.

Mankowitz and Harwick exchanged glances and Harwick wondered, "What was that all about?"

Mankowitz shrugged and shook his hands, trying to get blood flow back to them. Since landing a few hours before, he hadn't been cold, but now that they weren't pushing forward or digging in, it was getting to him. Besides the artillery, there had only been the occasional rifle shots, mostly from the ridges surrounding Massacre Bay.

Mankowitz answered, "G Company's over there. They must've run into a worthy target, I guess."

Sergeant Jakant was moving from hole to hole and when he got to theirs, he asked, "You two got what you need?"

"Sure thing, Sergeant," Answered Mankowitz.

"We're moving out soon. The Nips are probably waiting for us up this here valley. G Company ran into some trouble on the east ridge, but nothing serious. I Company's running up the other side, but they've only seen discarded Jap stuff. No resistance. We'll move out in an hour, so get some food and make sure you've got plenty of ammo."

Harwick gulped loudly and asked, "We're attacking at night?"

Jakant scowled, "That a problem for you, Harwick? Need your beauty sleep or something?" Harwick shook his head and averted his eyes. Jakant added, "I'd rather get this shit over with quick. If it means moving at night, so be it."

An hour later Charlie Company rose like apparitions and moved up the valley. The wind had died down a little, but the sky still spit icy rain into their faces. Even in the shifting fog, there was no chance of getting lost. Steep slopes surrounded the valley. If you nudged up against one, you couldn't go any further.

Mankowitz was glad to be moving. Tents hadn't made it ashore yet, and sleeping on the cold, wet ground wasn't something he was looking forward to. He'd rather patrol than try to sleep in his miserably cold foxhole.

The valley gradually rose in elevation. Streams drained small lakes, which the company skirted on either side. More than a few soldiers stepped into holes and sank up to their armpits in black, oily mud. Cursing marked their locations like beacons.

The valley steepened, and soon they were trudging through snow. The spread-out formation created too much lag, so Captain Smith ordered a single-file line. Mankowitz was in the center of the line and the pathway through the snow became muddy. His leather boots sank into it and squelched as he trudged along. He could feel wetness seeping in. He wondered how the hell he'd ever dry them out.

The snow lit up the darkness somewhat, and despite the cloud cover and wispy fog, Mankowitz could see pretty well. The ridges rising to either side were impressive. He couldn't see the tops, but he got a sense of how steep they were. He had no doubt the GIs up there were having to deal with much lower temperatures and probably bitingly cold winds. It wasn't so bad down here.

The fog suddenly lifted, drifting with the wind. The

company was spread out along a wide swath of snow, their black silhouettes stood out starkly against the white background. They approached the top of the pass and Mankowitz eyed it suspiciously. If there were Japs up there, they couldn't help but see them. He noticed other soldiers looking around nervously. With the fog gone, he felt hopelessly exposed.

His fears were realized when gunfire shattered the stillness. Mankowitz froze for a moment, thinking it sounded like a crazed woodpecker. Snaps and pops around his ears made him flinch.

"Get down!" Someone yelled.

He snapped from his momentary trance and dropped onto the muddy path. Oily mud splashed onto his face and the odd smell of it filled his nostrils. He heard men screaming but couldn't decide if they were screams of agony or fear.

More machine guns joined in and he couldn't determine their locations. They sounded as though they were all around him. Was that possible? He lifted his head, trying to get a look. He saw dots of light to his front, but also to either side. The air overhead buzzed, as though alive with swarms of killer bees. Would the snowbank he cowered behind stop a bullet?

As though in answer, Private Guittierez laying down in front of him suddenly lurched and grunted heavily. Mankowitz stared into the murky darkness. He could only see the soles of Guittierez's size eleven boots. He crawled forward and tapped his leg, "Guty! Hey Guty! You okay?" There was no answer.

He crawled until he was beside him. He pushed him onto his back and even in the sooty darkness he could see his staring, lifeless eyes. He pulled back in alarm and his gloved hand came away wet and sticky. He stared at the gloves his mother had given him. Panic rose in his craw. He screamed, "M—Medic! Medic! Guty's hit."

Behind him, Harwick yelled, "We've gotta get out of here, Mank." He rose onto his knees and fired his M1 in the direction of the muzzle flashes. His clip pinged and he dropped back into the mud. The bullets snapping overhead intensified and Mankowitz snugged up to Guittierez. He felt the sickening impact of bullets smacking into his dead body. He yelled, "Stop firing, you asshole! They see your muzzle flash."

Just as quickly as it started, the firing stopped. Mankowitz could hardly catch his breath and his hands were shaking uncontrollably. He slowly lifted his head and looked behind him. He could see Harwick's outline, but he wasn't moving. He called out, "Harwick! You okay?"

Harwick looked up and gave him a thumbs up. "Yeah, I'm fine. Why'd they stop?"

Mankowitz risked lifting his head again and saw the reason. "The fog's come back. I can't see the ridge anymore."

Lieutenant Hubert ordered, "Fall back! Spread out and find some cover."

Mankowitz got to his knees and leaned down to check on Guittierez again. He wasn't moving and his chest glistened with wetness. He took a glove off his shaking hand and felt for a pulse. There was nothing there, and he quickly put the glove back on. "Guty's dead," he stated.

GIs were up and moving back, pushing their way past Mankowitz. "Give me a hand with Guty, will ya?" Harwick slung his smoking M1 and helped lift Guittierez's dead weight. They struggled a few yards as soldiers streamed past them. A slow sizzling sound overhead made Mankowitz pause and look up. An explosion thirty yards away flashed in the fog. More followed and Sergeant Calder yelled, "Mortars! Take cover."

They dropped Guittierez's body and dove into the beaten down path. Mankowitz held his helmet tightly to his head. The muffled explosions shook the mucky ground beneath him, and he imagined it must shimmy like chocolate pudding. The barrage continued but the rounds never got closer. The fog kept the spotters from correcting the fire, and it soon stopped.

Harwick pulled his dripping face out of the mud. Mankowitz could see the whites of his eyes, which looked like dinner plates. Harwick said, "Time's a-wasting. Let's get the hell outta here." Mankowitz glanced at Guittierez and Harwick smacked his arm, "He's dead. He won't mind spending the night out here. If that fog lifts again, we'll be cut to shreds."

Mankowitz nodded. The retreating column had bypassed them, and they were now the furthest forward and totally exposed. Below and to the right, there was a rock feature, and he could see GIs digging in around it. He pointed, "Let's get over there."

Harwick didn't need coaxing, and soon they were both high kneeing through the dirty snow. A GI saw them coming and raised his rifle. Harwick raised his rifle over his head and yelled, "Harwick and Mank coming in. Don't shoot for chrissakes." The GI averted his muzzle and they slid into the relative safety of the boulder pile.

When they got their breath back, Mankowitz found Sergeant Jakant. "Guty's dead. We had to leave him up the trail."

Jakant shook his head. "He ain't the only one. Patterson and Burrill bought it too." He pointed into the gloom at a soldier propped against a boulder. The medic, Private Hayward crouched in front of him, placing a bandage over a messy leg wound. "Peters got hit too. Not sure about the other squads."

A firefight broke out somewhere behind them, high on the ridge. The flashes in the fog were surreal. It was nearly impossible to tell how far away the distant pops and flashes were. From the valley floor, it looked as though the fight was taking place in mid-air.

Harwick took a long pull off his canteen, then sealed the lid. "This fog is something else."

Mankowitz agreed, "Sure saved our asses back there. They had us pinned, and those mortars would've wreaked havoc if they coulda seen anything."

3

———————

Private Hunter was straddling the knife-edged ridge line overlooking the west arm of Holz Bay. The rest of 3rd Squad was spread out behind him. Private Wilkes had been sent back to lead the rest of the company to them. The fog obscured the bay water, but that wasn't Hunter's focus. The canyon directly below the ridge led straight to their objective, Holz Bay. But there was a problem.

He handed the binoculars back to Staff Sergeant Rizzo. "I see what you see, Sergeant. The Nips are dug in about halfway up that ridge across the valley. From what I can see, they'll have clear fields of fire on us until we're in the bottom of the canyon."

Rizzo put the binoculars back to his eyes and adjusted them slightly. "Hoped I was just seeing things. There's no way to get into that canyon without them spotting us...at least in daylight. Captain Willoughby isn't gonna let us wait for dark. We're right on schedule and he won't do anything to put us behind if he can help it."

Rizzo's assistant squad leader, Sergeant Mavis added, "Now that we need the fog, it's gone."

Rizzo nodded and handed the binocs to Mavis. "She's a

fickle mistress, no doubt. I heard the transport plane a while ago so I'm not complaining about the lack of fog, though."

Mavis pointed back the way they'd come. "We could backtrack and slip into the canyon from the saddle back there. They'd still see us, but we'd be at the edge of their range." Rizzo nodded, evaluating the distance.

Hunter shrugged, "Or we could slide down from here."

Rizzo peaked over the side. The slope was at least thirty-five degrees and snow covered. "You mean like sled down it?"

Hunter nodded. "Sure. Our ponchos would work. The first few guys might be slow, but once there's a good track down, we'll fly. The Japs would have to get damned lucky to hit us, and they'd wouldn't have much time to adjust before we'd be in the canyon's cover."

Mavis peered over then pulled back. "It's damned steep. Japs wouldn't have to shoot us, the rocks at the bottom of the snow field would do the job for 'em."

Hunter hesitated. He wasn't in the habit of arguing with NCOs. Rizzo nudged him, "Speak freely, Private."

Hunter pointed down the slope. "The snow's icy up here, but halfway down it turns to slush. It's the same stuff we trudged through last night. If you get going too fast, just roll off the track and the soft snow will stop you soon enough."

Rizzo smiled, "I like it. I'll pass it by Willoughby."

The rest of the company filtered onto the ridge. They dispersed gear from the successful airdrop to the squad. Only one of the two scheduled planes showed up. It dropped food, ammunition, and a few sleeping bags. The pilot explained through a static-filled transmission that the other plane had engine trouble and had to return to Adak Island. Another flight with the rest of the supplies, including most of the sleeping bags, would come in the evening.

Staff Sergeant Rizzo explained the situation to Captain Willoughby and the other officers, along with Private

Hunter's suggestion. They decided they'd send two squads at a time, each creating their own sledding lane. The rest of the company would follow squad by squad until only one squad remained. Then they'd follow the canyon to the beach at Holz Bay.

They scouted out a likely descent route. The snow coverage was good and there weren't any obvious breaks or obstructions for them to career off or into. Hunter crouched behind Gentry and Private First Class Hammond. Hammond would go first. He'd insisted on it, saying he had more sledding experience than anyone else in the squad since he'd grown up sledding in Denver.

Hunter didn't think sledding required any special talent, but he didn't mind not leading. After all, the faster ride would come once they laid a good track down. He also didn't relish being the first to smash into an unseen fissure in the snowfield.

Captain Willoughby lowered the binoculars after gazing at the enemy positions across the valley. He barked, "A thin layer of fog's coming in. Go now."

PFC Hammond looked back at the others; excitement tinged with fear in his eyes. He laid his poncho out in front of him. His pack was snug on his back, along with his carbine. He leaned forward and pulled the front lip of the poncho up, so it would slide easier. He licked his lips, then threw himself over the edge. His body weight crushed through the layer of ice and his body stuck there. It would've been comical, had it not been for the enemy soldiers across the valley.

Hunter peaked over the edge, seeing Hammond's wide eyes staring back. "Give me a push," he pleaded.

Hunter nodded and leaned over, grabbing Hammond's boots. "Lift the lip above the ice and I'll push you." Hammond arched his back, lifting the front of the poncho. Hunter pushed and Hammond's poncho went past the crushed lip of ice holding him in place. He slid away. Hunter watched as he picked up speed. Snow wafted over Hammond's helmeted head. Hunter pulled himself out of the way and Gentry leaped onto the track and was soon gaining on Hammond.

More and more squad members flung themselves over the side. The far-off sound of a woodpecker caught his attention and he looked across the valley. The thin fog had lifted, and he could see the winking flashes of enemy machine guns and rifles. Geysers of snow leapt up, trying to catch up with the sliding GIs.

He ducked beneath the ridge and got in line. When it was his turn, he flung himself onto the well-worn track and followed his comrades headfirst down the slope. The speed was exhilarating, and the zipping of bullets and exploding geysers of snow made it even more exciting. He couldn't stop himself from whooping. He wasn't the only one.

Twenty-five hundred feet flashed by in under a minute. He didn't want it to end, but the bottom of the canyon was approaching fast. Huge sprays of wet snow erupted in front of him as soldiers rolled off the track and somersaulted though the soft snow.

He rolled left, hoping the man in front had gone right. His backpack dug into the snow and he back flipped three times before finally stopping. He was dazed but smiling. He saw the next man coming fast. He dove out of the way as PFC Runyon smashed and rolled into the spot he'd just vacated.

Sergeant Mavis was next, and he waited an instant too long to bail. He plowed headfirst into the wall of snow piled at the bottom of the canyon. He thrashed and struggled, his body firmly planted. He had to be pulled out by two GIs who could barely contain their laughter.

They lay two more tracks down and soon the majority of the company was in the canyon and out of the enemy gunner's sights. The Japanese fired mortars. The small explosions bracketed the sledding paths, which were etched into the snow in stark relief.

Gentry slapped Hunter's back, "Glad we didn't have to sled through that."

Hunter nodded, "Did you see Willoughby come down? The old geezer was grinning ear to ear and hollerin' like a damned cowboy on a bronco."

For a few minutes they felt like kids. Their moods changed quick when the mortars marched steadily down the hill toward them. "Take cover!" Yelled Lt. Wilcox.

Hunter's squad pushed deeper into the canyon until they came to the little creek trickling down the center. There wasn't much cover, just a few boulders and the soft edges of tundra that had been worn away by the creek water.

Sergeant Rizzo ordered, "Dig in."

The mortar shells were soon landing among them, ripping tundra, and sending deadly shrapnel in every direction. Hunter felt as though his teeth would rattle from his head. A screeching whistle, then a thud directly in front of him almost made him lose his bowels. The barrage finally stopped, and he slowly raised his helmeted head out of the burbling creek.

Three feet in front of him, a mortar shell hissed and sizzled. It was halfway buried in the creek. A dud, he thought. But then his mind whirred like a top, more likely a delayed fuse.

Without taking his eyes off it, he backed away quickly. He backed into something soft. He turned and saw the smoking remains of a soldier. He couldn't identify who it was, it was simply a mass of parts, glistening and bloody against the brown tundra grass. He pushed past it until he was far enough away from the unexploded mortar shell. He struggled to catch his breath.

Men were moving, getting to their feet, and dusting themselves off. There was moaning and a few calls for the medic. From the top of the small hill protecting them from the enemy machine guns, rifle fire erupted. Geysers of water splashed him, and he rolled into an embankment. Bullets smacked the ground and ricocheted off boulders.

Hunter pulled his carbine off his shoulder and for the first time, aimed it at the enemy. He could see helmeted heads popping up near the top of the low hill and firing down upon them. He fired just as his target dropped back into cover. He waited; he would come back up once he'd chambered another round. Other targets presented themselves, but he stayed steady. Finally, the space over his sights filled with a Japanese head and he pulled the trigger. The carbine's .30 caliber pistol ammo didn't pack as much of a punch as the M1 Garand or the .45 caliber Thompson that the NCOs brandished, but it did the job. The Japanese soldier's head snapped back and dropped out of sight.

He moved to the next target and fired again. The near miss sent dirt into the soldier's face, and he hoped he'd blinded the son of a bitch. Someone had seen him, and a bullet whizzed past his ear. He ducked beneath the lip and wiggled his way up the creek a few yards before rising again.

He had an even clearer shot. A soldier's entire torso appeared. He was rearing back to throw a grenade. Hunter fired three times and the front of the soldier's tunic turned red and he dropped out of sight. He heard a muffled explosion and dust and debris rained down around the trench line. He whooped.

The firing slackened, but he kept his sights steady, waiting for more. The wind kicked up and it started sleeting. As if someone had pulled a curtain, the ridge line, along with the enemy soldiers, was suddenly out of sight. Hunter was immediately wet, and the wind made him shiver, despite the adrenaline coursing through him like an out-of-control freight train.

Orders were passed, and although he couldn't see more than a few yards, the company moved upstream until they rounded a bend in the canyon. There was more cover here. The bend created a collecting point for whatever detritus came from upstream. A few boulders pushed up against the wall, forming shallow caves and depressions. It wasn't dry, but it was out of the wind and more importantly, out of view from enemy guns.

They dug in along the line and Captain Willoughby made it his CP for the time being. The ridge they'd sledded down loomed on their left, the low hill with the newly occupied trench line was on their right. In front of them, the canyon stretched about a mile all the way to Holz Bay. Hunter wondered what that mile was going to cost them in blood.

CHARLIE COMPANY INCHED their way forward up the steepening slope toward Jarmin Pass. The roar of the 105mm Howitzers rolled over them and seemed to ripple through the thick, wet air. Flashes through the fog and darkness showed them the top of the pass they were creeping towards. It was getting ever closer.

The occasional crack of a rifle or the hammering of an enemy machine gun kept them cautious. They couldn't see the enemy and hoped they couldn't see them.

Private Mankowitz stayed close to Private Harwick's back. He didn't like being so bunched up, but Lieutenant Hubert insisted the men buddy up so no one would wander. Getting lost in the fog would be as simple as losing sight of the soldier in front of you for more than a few seconds. Calling out would draw enemy fire and backtracking might end in a friendly fire incident. Whether you were shot by the enemy or one of your own men—the results were the same.

Harwick stopped and hunched in the snow. Mankowitz nearly bumped into him. Men behind stopped and hunkered all the way down the line. The platoon was moving up the valley in six different single-file lines. Mankowitz's line was on the left flank. He couldn't see it, but off to his left a few yards, the slope to the ridge loomed. He knew I Company was up there somewhere trying to push to the saddle in coordination with Charlie. G Company was doing the same thing on the opposite ridge.

The mauling they'd taken a few hours earlier kept them vigilant and hyper-aware. They'd stowed their dead and wounded in a dug-out snow cave that became their temporary CP. They hoped they wouldn't have to wait too long to get the wounded out. The platoon medic, Private Hayward, stayed with wounded, which didn't help Mankowitz's confidence.

The volume of fire from the three Howitzers decreased. They only fired once every ten minutes. The flashes served as markers of the enemy's position. The 81mm mortars halfway up the east ridge were ready to provide support to anyone that gave them a firing solution. The heavy weapons platoon was with them, their .30 and .50 caliber machine guns facing Jarmin Pass.

Tense minutes passed before Harwick moved again. There was no explanation for the delay, he simply stopped because the man in front of him stopped. Mankowitz felt the cold seeping into his bones. He hadn't truly been warm since leaving California. Despite being in the middle of a platoon of men, he felt alone and vulnerable.

They'd been creeping up the valley for an hour, and Mankowitz felt like they were well beyond where they'd first made contact during their first attempt. He sensed they were close to the top, but he couldn't pinpoint anything concrete. The flash and crump of a 105mm shell lit up the fog. He was astounded by how close they were.

Lieutenant Wilcox hissed an order and the column stopped again. They passed the word up the line to dig in quietly. This was as far as they were going until the fireworks started on the flanks. They spread out, wondering when things would kick off.

Mankowitz shucked his pack and pulled his entrenching tool out. Digging in the dirty snow was easy enough and cutting through the tundra grasses beneath was a breeze but going much deeper would put him into the mud and beyond that the hard frozen layer.

Once he deemed the hole deep enough, he hunkered and blew warm air into his gloved hands. He checked his M1, made sure his ammo and grenades were easily accessible, then settled in as best he could. Harwick tucked in beside him, and he was grateful for his added body heat.

Sergeant Calder moved from hole to hole. Mankowitz could barely see the two soldiers huddled in the next hole only ten yards away. When Calder got to them, he said in a gruff voice, "Rest awhile but don't get too comfy. Soon as I and G company hit their flanks, the 81s will light 'em up with flares. That's our signal to move. Flares pop, you go. Got it?"

"Got it, Sergeant," mumbled Mankowitz.

"How we supposed to see anything in this fog?" asked Harwick. Calder shrugged and moved off without answering.

A half hour passed. Mankowitz and Harwick shivered beside each other. Harwick whispered, "Wish we'd get this thing started for crying out loud. Freezing my ass off."

Mankowitz nodded, "Funny, isn't it? I feel the same way, but once it starts—we'll probably wish it hadn't."

"Jesus, Mank. You a philosopher now?" Another 105mm shell slammed into the saddle. The flash was brighter; the fog had thinned. Harwick shook his head, "How long's this night gonna last? It feels never-ending."

Mankowitz grinned, "Who's the philosopher now?"

Fire erupted from the west ridge, but instead of being near the saddle it was much farther back. The volume intensified. The fog had thinned, they could see flashes and red tracer rounds crisscrossing.

Mankowitz was aghast, "That all the further they got? They're supposed to be up here with us."

The woodpecker sound of multiple enemy machine guns from the eastern ridge joined in, and tracer rounds sliced across the valley and engaged I Company.

Harwick's face was lit by the muzzle flashes and tracers. "Shit, they're all behind us. This is not good."

More fire joined along the eastern ridge. Green and yellow tracer fire cut into the enemy machine guns shooting across the valley. Mankowitz pointed, "That's gotta be G Company getting in on it. You're right; we're way the hell out front. If they spot us, we'll have them on three sides."

Harwick spit then said, "Hope Captain Smith's got the sense to have us fall back."

A few minutes passed and the firefight happening along the ridges was like watching some bizarre 4th of July celebration. Suddenly a series of bright flares burst over the top of the saddle. They floated lazily beneath small parachutes, descending through layers of thinning fog.

"Aw shit," Harwick complained.

The heavy machine guns flanking the 81mm mortars opened fire on the saddle and were immediately met with multiple streams of Japanese return fire. Lieutenant Hubert stood and waved them forward. "That's it. Let's go. Move up. Bound and cover."

Harwick and Mankowitz got to their feet and took tentative steps. Mankowitz's joints were cold and stiff, and he grimaced with each step. The snow wasn't as thick on the edges and they made good progress. The machine gun duel overhead, combined with the sputtering flares, lit up the dirty snow.

Mankowitz's heart was in his throat; he could see the silhouettes of enemy soldiers just seventy yards away. There was a long line of them, all aiming and firing toward the ridges and heavy machine guns. The sustained flashes and long tongues of fire marked the enemy machine gun positions. There looked to be a hell of a lot of them.

They hadn't been spotted yet. Perhaps they wouldn't see them at all. Perhaps they could walk right up on 'em and kill them in their trenches. That pipe dream ended when a startled yell from the trench line focused the enemy on Charlie Company. At first it was only rifle fire.

Mankowitz dropped to a knee and aimed over his sights at an enemy's helmeted head. He fired and the kick of his weapon felt good. He steadied his aim and fired again. His target dropped out of sight. He did not know if he'd hit him or just made him duck. He moved his muzzle left and fired again and again. GIs moved up and he continued firing, keeping the enemy's heads down.

The eight-round clip pinged, and he quickly inserted a new one. Harwick sprinted forward and before he knew what he was doing, Mankowitz was running too. Bullets snapped past his ears and he dove forward. Something tugged at his arm. He ignored it and rolled into a slight defilade. More parachute flares burst over the Japanese lines, silhouetting them nicely.

Mankowitz was ten yards closer to them. He pushed his rifle through grass sticking up from the snow. In the light from the flare, he saw a Japanese soldier's torso lift above the trench line. He was aiming a long rifle at the advancing GIs to Mankowitz's right. Mankowitz adjusted and fired. He pulled the trigger in quick succession and the soldier spun as the powerful 30.06 rounds pierced his chest.

Harwick slapped his shoulder and got to his feet again. He ran forward and Mankowitz cursed and fired in the general direction of the trench, trying to give him cover. Harwick hurled himself into the next depression. Mankowitz couldn't see him and hoped he'd made it. Bullets whipped the air overhead, and it pockmarked the snow with geysers, forcing him to duck and reload.

He thumbed in a fresh clip and glanced right. GIs were moving up and making excellent progress. The covering fire from the heavy machine guns on the east ridge was keeping most of the enemy machine guns occupied. Explosions rocked the slope and Mankowitz wondered if the Japanese were hitting them with mortars again.

"Here I come!" he yelled. He heard Harwick firing as he got to his feet, ran a few yards, and hurled himself forward. More GIs piled into the depression. In the darkness it was difficult to tell who who was.

A new sound from the top of Jarmin pass gave them pause. Bright flashes exploded over the top of the mortar crews and machine gunners halfway up the eastern ridge. The popping blasts reverberated throughout the valley and sounded like amplified bursts of popcorn.

"What the hell's that?" someone yelled.

Someone else answered, "The Japs got an ack-ack gun!"

The fire from the friendly machine guns stopped. The sudden lack of fire was like losing a security blanket. The ack-ack bursts continued lighting up the heavy weapons platoon in ghastly flashes. Quick views of smoke and darting shapes was all Mankowitz could see.

The air overhead suddenly came alive with machine gun fire. The Nambus, freed from the suppressing fire from the ridges, chopped away at the advancing GIs. The last sputtering flares from the 81mms landed and extinguished, plummeting them into darkness.

Mankowitz rose, but ducked when bullets smacked the lip of snow he huddled behind. Without the flares it was utterly dark. The only light came from muzzle flashes and grenade explosions. The advance stopped. The enemy machine guns poured a steady dose of lead into them. The firefights along the ridges seemed to abate. There was less and less tracer fire from friendly troops.

The clang of a bullet smashing into metal made the soldier

beside Mankowitz curse a blue streak. He recognized Private Lance's voice. "You hit, Lance?" he asked.

Lance held up his helmet. It had a jagged crease over the top. "That came from behind us!" He chucked the ruined helmet down the snowfield and it slid into the darkness. The GIs tried to make themselves as small as possible.

Sergeant Jakant's voice pierced the darkness. "You men up there, fall back! Stay low. We'll cover you."

Shells from the Howitzers slammed into the enemy positions, but the incoming enemy fire didn't diminish. Mankowitz and the others crawled as fast as they could as bullets whizzed in both directions only feet overhead. Explosions rocked the slope as Japanese grenades hurled from the trenches rolled downhill and exploded. They were too far away to do much damage, but they added to the chaos.

The GIs got to Sergeant Jakant's line of soldiers. "Anyone wounded?" he asked.

Mankowitz shook his head, "Don't think so."

Jakant raised his voice, "Captain wants us off this hill before the Nips behind us on the ridges decide to cut us off. The cannon cockers are gonna fire smoke. That'll be our signal to fall back."

"Where's the fucking fog when we need it?" exclaimed Private Lance.

The firing died down gradually. The darkness hid them for now. Smoke shells popped and enveloped the pass. The occasional muzzle flash pierced through. Jakant and Sergeant Calder pushed them down the hill, "Go! Don't stop till you get to the CP."

4

The fog settled into the canyon which Hunter and the rest of Scout Company huddled in throughout the rest of the day and into early evening. There'd only been the occasional rifle exchange with unseen enemies since they'd moved to their makeshift CP.

The droning of an aircraft overhead made them all look up hopefully. Two squads had stayed on the ridge, hoping to receive another air drop. Hunter hoped it wasn't as foggy up there as it was down here.

Private Gentry shook his head, "If it's even half as foggy up there, I don't see how they'll make the drop."

"Flares?" asked Hunter.

Gentry shrugged, "Maybe, but the fog will hide those too."

The droning of the aircraft engine lasted for a half hour. It would fade, then grow, then fade again. Finally, as darkness enshrouded them, it faded into nothingness.

Sergeant Rizzo emerged from the gloom with bad news. "The boys on the ridge radioed. The plane didn't make a drop that they could see. It's as thick up there as it is down here." There were groans and low curses. He held up his hands for quiet and continued. "This might not be as quick a job as we thought. There're no guarantees about getting resupplied either. The thirty-second landed at Red Beach a day late," he pointed northeast. "Captain has spotty contact with them. He doesn't know much beyond the fact that they landed. They could be here tomorrow or a week from now…just depends on the Japs.

"Our job hasn't changed, though. The more we keep the Nips looking our way, the easier time those boys on the beach will have, and the quicker we'll link up." He took out a cigarette and the flare of his lighter lit up the fog. He took a long drag and blew it out slow. "In case we don't get a resupply, Captain's ordered half-rations." There were more groans. "We gotta make what we have last. Understand?"

"Yes, Sergeant," they answered.

Hunter asked, "What're we gonna do about those Japs on the near ridge?"

Rizzo smiled, "Glad you asked, Hunter. We can't move down the canyon until we deal with 'em. Willoughby's been in contact with the 7th Recon. They're a mile or so northeast of us. They're gonna push onto the ridge overlooking our little problem and if the fog allows it, engage them from above. Meanwhile, we'll be coming from below. We'll also have mortars ready to help." He looked at the glowing dials of his watch. "Since it's too damned cold to sleep, Willoughby wants us to move out before it gets light. Be ready to move at 0200. Fill your canteens but remember to ration food. We gotta suck it up until we're resupplied."

Hunter filled his canteen upstream of the CP. The fog felt like a wet blanket draped around him. It was a bizarre sensation to be only yards away from people yet feel as alone as if he were on the moon. The darkness, coupled with the snow and fog, was surreal. He was used to the confines and limited visibility of a forest, but this was different. What would keep them from walking straight into a Jap machine gun nest? The thought circled through his head for the next few cold, miserable hours.

At 0130 Hunter and 3rd Platoon huddled outside the CP. Captain Willoughby himself briefed them. He stood at the base of the largest boulder and raised his voice. Hunter was a few yards away from him and could just barely see his outline. The thick air muted his normally booming voice. "Stay close together. I don't want anyone getting lost in this soup. And remember, don't engage the enemy until you can see something. The Seventh Recon boys will be in the area by daybreak. Let them engage and when the Nips are turned the wrong way, roll 'em up." It was brief and to the point. He'd leave the details up to Lt. Wilcox. "Questions?"

Sergeant Mavis asked, "What if the fog doesn't thin out, sir?"

Lieutenant Wilcox stepped forward and fielded the question. "If I may, sir?" Willoughby gestured the affirmative, and Wilcox addressed the question. "I'll make the call. If we stumble into 'em before the 7th arrives, we'll attack. They're just as blind as we are."

Private Lance leaned close to Hunter's ear and whispered, "Yeah, but they're dug in and we're in the open."

Wilcox continued, "Bring extra grenades and ammo. If it comes down to it, lead with grenades and follow with carbines. You NCOs with the Thompson's—they don't call 'em trench sweepers for nothin."

The platoon made their way to the base of the slope leading toward the enemy trench line. It was impossible to get an exact fix in the darkness and fog, so they guessed and moved slowly upward. The snow was deeper near the bottom and soon men were straining and breathing hard as they plowed their way through as quietly as possible.

Hunter could see a few GIs behind him. He was on point, but that only meant he was ten yards further ahead. Any farther and he'd be invisible and alone. He tried to picture the morning firefight. How far away had they been? How long would it take to climb to the trench?

He figured the trenches were maybe 150 yards above them. Lt. Wilcox wanted the platoon to stay on their left flank, so they'd started their slow climb directly from the CP. Hunter figured that would put them about 100 yards up the canyon from them. But what if the Japs had more than one trench line? What if they were waiting for them with their fingers on those damned machine gun triggers? And wouldn't this trajectory put them directly in 7th Recon's fire?

He shook his head—he only needed to concentrate on seeing what was directly in front of him. Seeing the enemy before they saw him would give him and the rest of the platoon, the best chance of surviving. He gulped, feeling the responsibility of the entire platoon upon his shoulders. He wished it was only himself he needed to worry about.

THE HIGHER HUNTER led them up the wind-scoured hillside, the thinner the snow layer became. The fog was still thick, but at least the walking was easier. With each step, he felt he was pushing his luck. How far did Lt. Wilcox expect them to go? It was difficult to gauge, but he thought the trench line must be close.

He stepped around a thicker patch of snow then turned and searched for the others. He nearly panicked when he didn't see anyone at all, not even the faint fuzzy outline of a GI. How long had it been since he last checked? He shook his head and took a deep breath.

His father used to tell him, 'if you get lost in the woods, don't panic. Once you let panic take root, you've signed your own death warrant.' His father, an accomplished woodsman, spoke from experience. He'd been on more than one search and rescue mission, looking for lost souls in the forests and craggy mountains of Montana. Invariably, the ones that lived to tell the tale, hadn't panicked but used their wits to make it easier for the searchers to find them.

The overwhelming urge to call out, passed. It hadn't been more than a few minutes since he'd last seen the other soldiers. They must be close, just out of sight. He hunched beside a snow patch and split his time between watching uphill for enemy soldiers and downhill for GIs.

Two minutes passed. It was time to retrace his steps and find the platoon. He hated doing even that. He might be mistaken for an enemy soldier. He eased down the hill, placing his feet into his own tracks. When he'd gone ten yards, there was a challenge from the mist, "Stone."

Hunter stopped and immediately answered, "Barricade." The native-Japanese English speakers had trouble pronouncing the letter r, so even if they knew the password, barricade would come out, *ballicade*.

"That you, Hunter?"

"Yeah, it's me. Why'd you guys stop?"

"Wilcox wants to send a team up from here and see if they can find the Japs without exposing the entire platoon."

Hunter knelt beside PFC Nunes. "Whatever happened to waiting for Seventh Recon?" he whispered. Nunes shrugged. Hunter asked, "Who's he sending?"

"Not us; team from 1st Squad."

Hunter expelled a breath he didn't realize he'd been holding. "I thought sure it'd be us again."

"No such luck. Follow me. Wilcox wants to hear from you."

Nunes led him to Lt. Wilcox. There was a hint of light in the east, but with the fog, it was more of a feeling than actually seeing direct light.

Wilcox lifted the rim of his helmet. "See anything up there, Hunter?"

He shook his head, "Nothing past a few yards. Feels like we must be getting close though, sir."

Wilcox nodded, "Agreed. I figure we're within sixty yards or so. I'm sending a team forward to check." Hunter adjusted his carbine and looked at his boots. Wilcox noticed his agitation and asked, "Something you wanna say, soldier?"

The 7th Scout Company prided itself on high caliber, tough training. The officers respected the common foot soldiers and vice versa. Everyone from the lowliest private to Captain Willoughby could speak their mind if they felt strongly about something. Hunter heard the challenge in Wilcox's voice, however, and thought better of making his opinion known. "No, sir."

Wilcox stomped away to give the order to 1st Squad. Hunter found his own squad and settled his ass into a partially dug out foxhole between Gentry and PFC Hammond. He placed his carbine across his lap and took a slug from his canteen.

Private Gentry elbowed him in the ribs. "How you doing?"

He twisted the lid back onto the canteen. "Don't feel good about 1st Squad trying to find the Nips. What's the point of orders if Wilcox isn't gonna follow 'em?"

PFC Hammond scowled, "He's not disobeying orders. He's trying to find them so we can assault them easier once it's light."

"I know he's not disobeying directly but look at this fog. You can't see five yards. If they find the Japs, the Japs can't help but find them too."

Hammond shrugged, "Maybe they'll hear 'em talking first."

Gentry guffawed, "At this hour; more like snoring."

Fifteen minutes passed like a slow drip from a leaky faucet. The cold seeped into Hunter's bones. He had been warm while taking point, but now he couldn't keep from shivering. He wondered how the wounded were faring. There were a few sleeping bags at the CP they could share, but that wouldn't be enough to keep them warm. What they needed was a blazing fire and a nice cozy enclosed space somewhere out of the elements.

His wandering mind was ripped back to the present by the sudden pop of a rifle, followed with the roar of a Thompson submachine gun on full automatic. The muzzle flashes were dim through the fog, but the contact was close. They all went onto their bellies and faced uphill with their carbines ready.

Staff Sergeant Rizzo was hustling past them. He hissed, "Tighten it up. Come closer. I'll see what's going on." More sporadic fire was suddenly punctuated with the unmistakable sound of a hand grenade exploding. It was impossible to tell if it was made in the USA or Japan.

More grenade explosions mixed with rifle and submachine gun fire, and Hunter hunkered lower. The woodpecker sound of an enemy MG firing a long, sustained burst, pierced the night. Tracers sliced through the fog and ricocheted wildly in all directions. The large muzzle flash marked the enemy trench line. It was closer than he figured it should be. Perhaps 1st Squad had stumbled into a new, closer enemy position.

There was yelling and cursing filtering through the fog. American voices mixed with harried Japanese voices as more fire was exchanged. Rizzo returned and told them to stay put for now but keep their eyes open.

Close yelling made them all aim their weapons toward the voice. It sounded American, but they'd been warned on the boat ride from San Francisco that there were plenty of Japanese that could speak very good English.

Someone yelled the challenge word, "Stone." There wasn't an immediate answer, just the thumping of feet. "Stone—or I fire!" the challenger's voice quavered.

Finally, there was an answer, "Barricade! Barricade! For Chrissakes, don't shoot. Six of us coming in."

Hunter wanted to collapse into the center and hear what was going on, but there could be enemy soldiers right on their tails or they could try for a flanking end-around. The Squad kept their carbines steady and watched their sector.

The harried voice of Sergeant Morganlander was loud, but Hunter couldn't make out all the words. The only thing he was sure of was that Morganlander had many colorful words for the enemy soldiers up the hill.

Sergeant Rizzo returned from the sergeant's tirade and told them what he'd learned. "Morganlander stumbled onto the Jap trenches. He didn't even see it until a Jap fired on him. He said his team returned fire and exchanged grenades with 'em but he doesn't know if they got any. Morganlander got creased across his cheek, but by some miracle, no one else was hit."

Sergeant Mavis asked, "So what now?"

"You're not gonna like it," he whispered. Everyone stared and he finally uttered, "The lieutenant wants to retreat thirty yards and cross in front of 'em then hit 'em from the other side."

Mavis shook his head, "Thought it'd be something like that."

Rizzo shrugged, "I know it's not the original plan, but if we can pull it off, we might surprise 'em. For all they know, that was just a patrol. They'll be awake but looking the wrong direction. I told him I agreed with his plan."

Mavis asked, "What about waiting for 7th Recon?"

Rizzo shook his head, "He doesn't want to play odds on the fog dissipating and thinks it'll actually help the attack he's planning. Now that we know where they are…" he squinted into the fog and ever-lightening world, "We can sneak on 'em better." Rizzo slapped Hunter's arm, "He wants you leading the platoon again. You up for it?"

Hunter gulped against a suddenly dry throat. "Of course, Sergeant. I'm ready."

"Okay then. If anyone's gotta piss or shit, now's the time. We leave in ten minutes."

Mavis asked, "Why the delay?"

Rizzo answered with mirth in his voice, "I think Morganlander might've shit his pants. A little cleanup's in order."

Mavis shook his head, "Can't wait to razz him about that."

"I wouldn't, if you know what's good for you, Jack," he said, his voice taking a serious tone, but he couldn't keep the smile off his face. "He'll probably never hear the end of it."

TWENTY MINUTES LATER, Hunter was leading the platoon back up the hill, only this time, they approached from the enemy's right flank. There was no way of knowing how far the trench extended, but they knew approximately how high it was from their last contact. His senses were tingling and on high alert. Hearing how Sergeant Morganlander and his team hadn't even seen the trench until the enemy soldier fired, sent a chill up his spine. His survival depended upon spotting them first.

He figured he'd made up the thirty yards they'd retreated and added another fifty. He was either slightly above the trench line or even with it. He stopped and signaled the man behind him to come up. It was Sergeant Mavis. He came up silently. Hunter signaled that he thought it was time to move laterally. Mavis nodded and held up a hand for him to wait. Soon the rest of the platoon was moving up and spreading out.

It was definitely getting lighter, but the fog was as thick as ever, giving the day a grayish look and feel. Water dripped from Hunter's helmet and off his nose. He felt as though he were living on the inside of a flushing toilet bowl with the lid shut. The wind increased and he wondered if it had anything to do with the rising sun. So far, he couldn't see any pattern between the time of day and the fog and wind. Both happened seemingly at random.

The Alaskan scouts had told them about the Williwa Winds which could—without warning—race down the hillsides toward the sea at well over 100mph. There was some—geologic/meteorologic/oceanic relationship causing the phenomenon, but the bottom line was, the wind could knock you off your feet and it was impossible to predict.

He closed his eyes tight and reopened them quickly. Focus, focus, focus. He moved forward, making sure of each footfall as though he were walking through a minefield. The GIs spread out in a V formation behind him. Down the hill another twenty yards, he knew another point man moved along carefully. He couldn't see him, but the company had practiced and trained enough to know the drill and would be within a few feet—forward or back from one another.

Hunter took long, slow strides. The fog shifted and rolled down the hill in front of him. All night, it had been as still as a tomb, but now it was moving. Not thinning—just moving. In the gray light, it looked like apparitions in long flowing gowns were floating into the canyon. It would be mesmerizing if he wasn't worried about dying.

He heard something ahead. He froze and held up his fist. It took a moment for Sgt. Mavis to see the signal, but when he did, he stopped and passed it down the line. Hunter slowly brought his carbine to his shoulder, but didn't put his eye to the sight. Had he really heard something, or was it his imagination getting the best of him? There it was again. He'd definitely heard voices, like low murmuring.

He stayed scrunched in a ball, his carbine aimed toward the phantom voices. There was more than one, he realized, and they were close—maybe twenty yards. He couldn't see anything but shifting fog, snow, and dripping grasses.

Mavis came up beside him. Without a word, Hunter touched his ear and pointed. Mavis listened for five minutes, but there was nothing. He looked questioningly at Hunter, and Hunter gave him an exaggerated nod. He was sure. Mavis slunk back into the darkness. Hunter felt alone. An entire platoon surrounded him, but the old familiar feeling of being on the moon was undeniable.

The platoon moved up until they were ten men deep and stretched thirty yards downhill from Hunter's position. Mavis was beside him again and he signaled he should use grenades. Hunter nodded and placed his carbine in the dirty snow at his feet. He pulled a grenade off his battle harness and wrapped his index finger around the pin. He flexed his other hand around the ridges of the deadly explosive which gave it the nickname, pineapple.

Mavis held up five fingers. He counted down, curling one finger at a time until his hand was in a fist. Hunter pulled the pin. The sound was slight but sounded like thunder to him. He released the spoon and hurled the grenade toward where he thought the voices were, then scooped his carbine, and pulled it to his shoulder. He closed one eye, trying to save his sight from the coming flash. It was a wasted effort. The flash was barely visible through the fog. More explosions erupted, reminding him of a string of firecrackers popping off on New Year's Eve.

There were screams. Hunter saw darting shapes. They couldn't be anything other than enemy soldiers. He fired at them, moving his barrel side to side, sending lead into them as fast as he could pull the trigger. Mavis opened fire with his Thompson as he walked forward.

Hunter reloaded and followed a step behind. He didn't see more shapes, so he held his fire. Down the slope, the intensity of fire grew to crazy levels and it wasn't just the pops and heavy thumps of Thompsons...there was return fire.

Hunter saw the large muzzle flash of a machine gun. He couldn't see the gunner, but he didn't have to. He pulled another grenade. It was only thirty yards away. He pulled the pin and chucked a line drive directly at the muzzle flash. He followed it with .30 caliber from his carbine. He wasn't the only GI with the idea. Grenades exploded around the machine gun and it finally fell silent.

Mavis was charging and burning through another magazine on full automatic. Hunter caught up to him. The trench, which had been so well concealed by the fog, was now a gaping maw stretching out before him. Bodies lay in the shadows, some squirming, most immobile. Yellow-tinged smoke mixed with the fog and wafted and shifted around the ugly scar in the tundra. Hunter fired into the gyrating mass of bodies until his magazine ran dry.

GIs suddenly filled the trench and the sounds of men grunting as they clashed in life-or-death grapples was terrifying to hear. Agonized screams rang from the fog. Hunter reloaded and kept his smoking barrel ready, but the fight had moved beyond him.

Third Squad guarded the trench entrance while the rest of the platoon cleaned up any remaining resistance. The only shots were from the carbines. The enemy Type-98 Arisaka rifles were silent.

A jubilant Lt. Wilcox walked out of the gloom surrounded by grim and dangerous looking GIs. Hunter had never thought of them that way, but in that moment that was the only word to describe them. He didn't know if he looked as dangerous—he doubted it—but he was bursting with pride. The 7th Scout Company was his unit and by God, they'd just taught the Japs a thing or two.

5

———

Private Mankowitz huddled as close to the potbellied stove as possible without actually burning himself. The rest of the squad pushed in on either side and for the first time in a long time, he felt warm.

The attack on Jarmin Pass had failed. The dead and wounded were hauled back to the beach under the cover of fog and spitting rain. The rest of the night, the pass was hammered with 105mm Howitzers joined by naval guns from destroyers patrolling the outskirts of Massacre Bay.

Harwick hunched beside Mankowitz. He rotated his gloved hands in front of the heat as though slow cooking them. "Think they'll send us up there again today?"

Sergeant Jakant standing across from him nodded. "Probably this evening. I heard there was some progress along the western ridge, so at least the Japs will have to worry about their flank and can't hammer us coming up the front side."

Private Lance stomped his feet, trying to force circulation back to them. "We're going up the middle again? Didn't work so well the first time, Sergeant."

Jakant scowled at him, "I don't know what the captain's

got planned, but whatever it is, you'll damn well do it with a smile on your face, Private."

Lance showed him his palms, "Just making a comment, Sergeant."

Jakant grinned, "You'll suck it up, soldier."

The tent flap opened letting in a flurry of wind laced with cold wetness. The squad hooted and cursed at Private Montgomery. He yelled over their jeers, "Cookies say they've got hot food ready for us, but it won't stay that way long."

They hadn't eaten anything except K-rations, but none of them moved from the heat. Another head poked into the tent. Everyone stiffened hearing Lt. Hubert's voice. "Get your asses to the mess hall. We're hitting the pass again at 1500 hours. Be at my tent at 1430, Sergeant."

Jakant braced, "Yes sir." Hubert left and Montgomery gave a sheepish grin, then left too. The BAR man, PFC Numchenko, growled, "Giving us hot food before sending us up the hill? We must really be in for it."

Jakant stepped from the circle and hitched up his collar. "Shaddup Numbnuts. You don't want your portion, I'm sure you can find someone who will."

Numchenko's heavy brow furrowed. "It's Numchenko— not numbnuts, Sergeant Jakant."

The squad laughed and reluctantly left the heat and followed Sergeant Jakant out into the blustery, wet day.

Mankowitz shivered and pulled his scarf over his chin and nose. Once again, he silently thanked his mother. He felt the wind cut through his clothes and mumbled to Harwick beside him, "Could really use a heavy coat out here, for crying out loud."

Harwick guffawed, "Yeah, no shit. You'd think the Army would know it's cold in the Bering Strait."

The food wasn't gourmet by any means, but the oatmeal and grits was hot, and the inside of mess hall was out of the wind and felt almost muggy. The GIs of Charlie Company ate in stages, and when everyone was more or less satiated, they filtered back into their respective tents and readied themselves for the next attack on Jarmin Pass.

THE FOG WASN'T AS thick as they pushed towards Jarmin Pass this time. Streaks of actual sunlight shone through in spots, lighting up the dirty snow, leading toward the enemy defenses. The pass was shrouded in mist and Mankowitz hoped it stayed that way until they were off the open slope. The artillery and naval guns were silent. The distant sounds of fighting—cracks of rifles and the staccato of answering machine guns—wafted through the air.

Mankowitz's muscles were sore, but it felt good to be moving. With each step, he felt warmth returning to his extremities. They followed the tracks they'd left the night before. It was surreal, as though he were revisiting a crime scene. The rain and sleet made the tundra soft and men cursed as they broke through or stepped into mud-holes. More than a few had to be hauled from the sticky, black mud with help from fellow soldiers.

Mankowitz stepped carefully. The thought of falling into a wet morass of mud made him shiver. Even standing in front of the potbellied stove for eight hours hadn't completely dried him out, and he didn't want to have to start all over.

They made steady progress. The wind blew from the pass, straight into their faces. Once again, he wondered how the fog could stay in place despite the wind. It seemed to defy physics and all reason. The tundra gave way to dirty, wet snow. Their tracks were obvious from the night before.

The company spread out and moved slower as the terrain steepened and the Japanese defensive line loomed. Mankowitz noticed signs of battle. Wind-scoured body depressions in the snow, scraped out holes, and frozen empty shell casings sticking from the snow, made it look as though the battle had happened years before.

He kept his eyes on the pass. The fog still clung to it. Streaks of sunlight shone on the snowfield. If it wasn't for specter of looming violent death hanging over them, it might've been pretty.

So far, they hadn't been spotted, but Mankowitz wondered how much longer that could last. He looked to either side, seeing well-spaced GIs moving up the slope cautiously. Everyone was on edge. They gripped their weapon's as though they were shields against dragon fire.

Mankowitz glanced down the slope and saw Lt. Hubert forty yards behind him. How far would he let them get? He longed to hunker down and dig in before the Japanese spotted them and raked them with machine gun fire.

He placed his boot into an old boot print and wondered who it belonged to. Was the soldier still alive? Was it bad luck to step in a dead man's boot print?

The fog enveloped him as though embracing him in a weightless, wet hug. He could barely see the GIs on either side. He couldn't see anyone behind him. He kept his concentration forward. The last thing he wanted to do was stumble into a trench or machine gun nest.

The fog thickened, cutting his vision to ten yards. The comforting, hazy forms around him were gone. Panic gripped his gut. He had a nearly overwhelming urge to sprint back the way he'd come—back into the light. He forced himself to breathe. Panic would kill him. He crouched, keeping his muzzle pointed up the hill. There was no point continuing forward until he knew he wasn't alone. He'd wait until the others caught up or someone ordered him to proceed.

The cold seeped into him like death. The fog shifted in a constant dance of deception. He wished he was fighting the Krauts in North Africa right about now. He cursed the fates that put him on the slope of this godforsaken island on the edge of the world.

A voice from below made him focus and helped quell his rising panic. "Mank? Where are you?"

It was Harwick's voice. Mankowitz matched his voice level, "I'm here. Up here in the fog."

Harwick's slight frame came into view and Mankowitz waved at him. Harwick waved back, giving him a sideways grin. "Lieutenant wants us to hold up." He came up beside him and hunkered. He squinted into the fog. "Watching you disappear into the fog..." he shook his head, "Looked like you got swallowed up."

Mankowitz nodded, "Felt like I'd stepped off the edge of the world." Harwick pulled a chocolate bar from his pocket and offered him a piece. Mankowitz nearly dropped it but shoved it into his mouth. He savored the chalky treat as it slowly melted in his mouth. He mumbled, "What's the plan?"

Harwick shrugged, "Dunno. Just got the word to hold up."

"We've gotta be close. Hell, they could be yards away and we wouldn't know about it," Mankowitz whispered.

Harwick nodded, "This fog scares the hell outta me. I thought I'd considered fighting in all types of weather and terrain, but I never thought about fog."

Silent minutes passed. The fog swirled, sometimes revealing, sometimes hiding the slope ahead.

Finally, they got the word from their squad leader, Staff Sergeant Calder. "We're gonna move up to contact. Lieutenant thinks they might've bugged out."

Private Lance asked, "Why's he think that?"

Sergeant Jakant slapped his arm, "Shaddup and do as you're told."

Calder answered, "I Company pushed past the pass this morning and Hubert thinks the Japs left to keep from being flanked." He shrugged, "We're gonna test his theory." Private

Lance started to say something, but Calder cut him off. He pointed at Numchenko. "You and Montgomery be ready to lay down fire at the first hint of contact. Our job's finding them, not assaulting them."

Numchenko patted his heavy BAR. "I didn't haul her all the way up here for nothing, Sergeant. We'll be ready." Montgomery, his assistant, nodded his agreement.

Calder pointed at Private Lance. "You're so eager…take point."

Lance was about to argue that he was a grenadier not a damned point man but thought better of it after seeing Jakant's eyes spitting flames. He simply nodded, "Yes, Sergeant." He looked at the others, then moved up the slope.

Mankowitz and Harwick were next in line. The fog was thick as ever, making the entire world gray and cold. They kept Lance in sight, which meant they were only five yards behind. Harwick moved a few yards from Mankowitz and the next man back, Private Numchenko moved away from him until the entire twelve-man squad was spread out and moving uphill steadily.

The snow thinned and Mankowitz didn't see anymore boot prints or shell casings from the night before. It didn't make him feel better to know they were much closer to the enemy this time around. The smell of sulfur and gunpowder filled his nose, and he thought he must be smelling the results of the long barrage. Perhaps the Japanese had been obliterated. He doubted that was possible. Without spotters, the cannon cockers were guessing at best.

Lance disappeared and called out suddenly. Mankowitz put his M1 to his shoulder, searching. He released his breath when he saw Lance's head reappear over the lip of a crater.

Mankowitz blurted, "Criminy sakes, Gary. I thought you got shot."

Lance shook his head, "Fell into a bomb crater, I think."

Mankowitz advanced, keeping his rifle ready. Sure

enough, the snowy ground was gouged with a large crater. Tundra grass was uprooted, and the blond strands made it look as though they'd stumbled upon an unkempt barber shop.

The fog thinned, turning from a solid mass to wisps. More craters dotted the hillside, and for the first time, they got a good view of the top of the pass. Mankowitz took in a sharp breath and aimed his rifle at something twenty yards away. He pressured the trigger but at the last instant realized he wasn't aiming at an enemy soldier but a torn-up chunk of wood sticking from the tundra. It didn't help ease his fear. "Shit, bunker straight ahead," he gasped.

He ducked, expecting an onslaught of machine gun fire, but nothing happened. Sergeant Calder didn't look into their hole as he walked past them, aiming his Thompson, but hissed, "Looks abandoned. Come on. Cover us, Numchenko."

The sound of Numchenko pulling the bolt on his big weapon was reassuring. He flopped onto his belly, extended the bipod, and aimed at the bunker. Mankowitz caught his breath and calmed his beating heart, then stood and took in the scene. Gouges from artillery fire dotted the area. Long trench lines and well-concealed bunkers were everywhere. There were no enemy soldiers visible.

They moved slowly, their weapons at their shoulders, and spread out as they approached the first enemy hole. Calder signaled them to stop. He unclipped a grenade, pulled the pin and hurled it into the bunker as he yelled, "Fire in the hole."

Everyone flopped to their bellies. The explosion wasn't impressive but sent them all into action. Mankowitz pulled himself to a crouch, waiting for a target, but there was no response. Six GIs, with Sergeant Jakant leading, ran forward and disappeared into the smoking bunker. Mankowitz got to his feet, expecting to hear a clash of fire, but there was noth-ing. More GIs surged forward with him. Harwick took off running, charging the dirty gash in the snow. Mankowitz kept his rifle at his shoulder and trotted forward.

The shattered bunker held pieces of human bodies, but the grenade had only mixed the offal. The bunker had suffered a near miss from one of the 105mm Howitzers, killing everyone inside. Beyond it, the trench line was intact, but it was empty of enemy troops.

Lieutenant Hubert waltzed up the slope as though he owned the place. He tried the radio, but even though he had line-of-sight to the beach, he couldn't connect, so he sent a runner to tell command that Jarmin Pass was deserted.

With the squad on either side of him, they moved up to the top and looked out over the island. Fog still clung to the highlands, but the valleys and lower hills were easily visible. Smoke from distant clashes to the north mixed with the fog and there were occasional barks of rifles, but it was relatively peaceful. The wind wasn't quite as harsh, and it wasn't raining or snowing. Although Attu was a relatively small island, the terrain looked ominous from Jarmin Pass.

Calder stood beside the commander of 2nd Platoon and asked, "Where to from here, sir?"

Hubert pointed to the next valley and the next ridge. "Through there. The Nips must've retreated back that way. Doubt they've gone far."

The distant crack of a rifle followed the sickening thump of a bullet hitting flesh. They all dropped, and Staff Sergeant Calder yelled, "Sniper!" He noticed Hubert's body laying at a crazy angle and he crawled to him. "Lieutenant! Lieutenant, are you hit?" There was no answer. Calder pushed his fingers into Hubert's neck, searching for a pulse or a wound. His hand came away wet and dripping with blood. He lay nearly on top of him and looked into his face. Hubert's eyes were wide with surprise and pain. His mouth gaped open and closed like a fish out of water, but the only sound was gurgling as he drowned in his own blood. "Medic!" Calder yelled.

Hayward was already sliding in. He pushed Calder off and ripped Hubert's clothes away from the seeping wound. He reared back as blood poured from Hubert's neck in a thick funnel. He placed his gloved hand over the fleshy wound and pressed hard, but there was nothing he could do. Hubert's eyes turned glassy and his breathing stopped. The hot blood steamed off his body in sickening waves, adding to the wisps of fog. Hayward's voice was distant, "He's gone, Sergeant. Bullet hit an artery—nothing could've saved him." He took his gloves off and wrung the blood out like a dishrag. Blood dripped onto the dirty snow.

Calder fumed, "Damn that cock-sucking Jap to hell! Anyone see him?" No one answered and no one deigned to lift their heads to find out. Calder shook his head and yelled, "Stay down. We'll kill all these sons of bitches soon enough."

6

Private Hunter huddled in a foxhole nestled into the hillside overlooking the canyon that 7th Scout Company occupied. After taking the low ridge from the Japanese the night before, they tasked 3rd Platoon with holding it. So far, the Japanese hadn't tried anything. Hunter's position allowed him to look south across the large valley to the enemy occupied peaks beyond, and north across the canyon where 2nd Platoon occupied the ridge. Whenever the fog lifted, the Japanese peppered the GIs on the northern ridge with machine gun and sniper fire. Due to low ammunition supplies, they couldn't fire back.

Hunter liked the view from his foxhole, but not the exposure to the constant cold and wind. Fog plagued the view more often than not, and a few times he convinced himself that the Japanese were sneaking on his position. But nothing but wind, snow, and fog assaulted him.

The buzzing of an aircraft overhead made him look up. PFC Hammond in the next foxhole over jolted, as though he'd been sleeping. Hunter searched the sky as the plane's engine noise changed. It wasn't quite as foggy as it had been most of the day, and the tantalizing engine noise grew louder, raising their hopes of resupply. Hammond pointed, "There it is. I see it to the north."

Hunter turned and squinted. Sure enough, he saw the twin-engine plane flying low, directly at them. A flare from 2nd Platoon on the higher northern ridge lanced through thin layers of fog. From his position, it looked as though it might hit the low-flying aircraft, but it wasn't close. It did the job though. The plane turned toward the slope and went into a shallow dive. Machine guns from the Japanese on the valley floor and southern peaks opened fire. The plane was out of range, but the exposed GIs waving bright orange markers were a tempting target.

Hunter leveled his M1 carbine and fired off a few rounds toward the valley. Hammond scolded him, "Knock it off. You're just wasting ammo."

Hunter nodded, "I know I can't hit 'em, but maybe I'll draw their attention away from our guys."

"You want 'em to fire on us?"

"Sure, why not? They don't have a good angle on us."

Hammond shrugged and handed him his M1 Garand. "Here, use this. You're a better shot than I am, and you might actually do some damage with it."

Hunter took the more powerful rifle and adjusted the sights. He settled his cheek into the stock. It was a long shot, but he could see the line of Japanese hunkered in the trenches and bunkers firing toward 2nd Platoon. He found the spitting smoke of a machine gun and settled on the dark area beyond. He blew his breath out slowly and fired. The kick was much heavier than the carbine, but he was ready, and it felt good. He fired three carefully aimed shots, then paused and took his eyes from the sights. There was no discernible change in the enemy fire, but he was sure they'd felt his presence.

He readjusted and fired methodically until the clip

pinged. He handed it back to Hammond, and he reloaded it with a fresh eight-round clip. The Japanese machine gunner adjust his aim and soon the surrounding air was alive with bullets. They ducked into their holes; confident they couldn't be hit unless they exposed their heads.

Hammond cursed as the volume of fire increased, "Well, you got your damned wish, Mack."

Hunter nodded and pointed north. The plane was turning and slowly winging toward 2nd Platoon. The GIs were waving frantically. From the side of the aircraft came bushels of supplies. They crashed into the ridge with puffs of snow and tundra. The GIs swarmed over them like ants attacking a wounded fly. Another plane was right behind the first, and the process repeated.

The incoming fire died down to a trickle and Staff Sergeant Rizzo slid to the edge of Hunter's hole, "What the hell was that all about, Hunter?"

"Just trying to take some pressure off Second Platoon, Sergeant."

Rizzo watched the last plane disappear into the clouds. "Glad the flyboys finally found us. We were getting low on everything."

Hunter said, "Sure hope they dropped some sleeping bags. It's gonna be colder than a witches' tit up here tonight."

Rizzo nodded his agreement. "It was on the list, but everything's been so screwed up..." he shrugged, "Who knows? Anything they drop will help." Rizzo yelled toward Sergeant Mavis' hole, "Johnny, get your ass over here."

Sergeant Mavis hustled over and pulled his scarf off his cold, scruffy face. "Yeah? What's the scoop, Rizzo?"

Rizzo pulled a crumpled cigarette from his pocket and held it between his gloved fingers. Hammond pulled out a zippo and finally got it lit. Rizzo took a deep drag and blew it out slowly. "This is my last one. There'll be rations in the drop. I'll resupply my stash then." He took his eyes from the glowing tip and addressed them. "I got orders from Lieutenant Wilcox—we'll be attacking tonight. Us, along with Second Platoon, will push along the ridges while Fourth pushes down the canyon. First will stay with the CP and be in reserve. We'll fire down on any concentrations Fourth Platoon comes across. Second will do the same thing along the north ridge." He looked at the small group of shivering men. "We'll kick things off at 2000 hours. That should be enough time for the resupply to get to us, but conserve food and ammo in case that doesn't happen." The men nodded their understanding and he continued, "Spread the word to the others." He leveled his gaze at Hunter and pointed his cigarette at him, "No more shooting." Hunter gave him a quick nod and Rizzo continued, "If Fourth gets in over their heads, it'll be up to us to bail 'em out. We'll cover any withdrawal that needs to happen." He took another drag and savored the smoke. He blew it out quickly, "Get some food and rest and be ready to jump off at 1945 hours."

Once Rizzo left and Sergeant Mavis was out of earshot, Hammond stated, "Gonna be black out tonight."

Hunter nodded, "Be like fighting by Braille. I'm not sure what's worse, the fog or the darkness."

Hammond guffawed, "We'll have both, no doubt."

***

HUNTER LED 3rd Squad along the left side of the ridge. The night was dark and cold. The fog had lifted partially, but he could see a few yards in front of him. The canyon off his left shoulder, was black and appeared to be bottomless. Fourth Platoon was down there somewhere, but he couldn't see them. The northern ridge where 2nd Platoon advanced was easier to see, but Hunter still couldn't see any GIs.

PFC Hammond whispered to him, "Slow down. Remember the boys in Fourth won't have it so easy."

Hunter hissed back, "You think this is easy? I can't see more than a few yards. I could walk right by an entire regiment of Nips and wouldn't know about it."

Hammond added, "I'm just telling you what Rizzo told me to tell you, asshole."

Hunter flipped him the bird and Hammond gave him a wry smile, then blew him a kiss. Hunter slowed his pace to a crawl.

He followed the natural contours which led them downslope slightly. The walking was relatively easy. The snow wasn't deep and unlike in the valleys; the tundra was solid. There wasn't much cover to speak of, besides the darkness and he felt hopelessly exposed. If he bumped into an enemy trench or bunker, it wouldn't end well. The sound of battle drifted up from the western arm of Holz Bay. He didn't know if it was elements of the 32nd or the 17th slugging it out down there, but it was reassuring knowing they weren't alone out here.

He wondered if his friend, John Mankowitz was down there fighting. It would be great to meet up with him again. That was the plan after all, linking up with the GIs attacking along the shore of Holz Bay. He wondered how many Japanese were between them.

Firing from the bottom of the canyon pulled him from his wandering thoughts, and he crouched. Flashes from deep within the canyon sparked. Despite his slow trudge, the fire was behind them about fifty yards. He turned down the slope. The sparks and noise intensified as GIs up the canyon returned fire. Tracers suddenly ripped up the canyon and ricocheted crazily. Through the darkness and fog it was difficult to discern exactly what was happening, but it appeared to Hunter that his platoon was above and behind Japanese.

Over the din of combat, he heard Lt. Wilcox on the hand-held radio. The radios had given them fits since leaving the submarine, but Wilcox was in contact with someone and speaking in clipped tones.

The squad tightened up and Hunter was glad to see familiar faces. Wilcox signed off and talked with his sergeants. The fire from the canyon diminished. The Japanese machine gun spitting flame and tracer rounds a moment before was silent now, but Hunter remembered where it was in the darkness and kept his eyes on the spot.

Finally, Sergeant Mavis relayed their orders. "Wilcox couldn't raise the boys in the canyon but talked with 2nd Platoon. They're in contact with 4th and are coordinating their attack with them. We're to dig in here and see if they flush 'em this way." His eyes focused and he held up a stiff index finger, "Be sure it's a Jap before you fire."

Hunter pulled his entrenching tool for what seemed like the millionth time and dug into the side of the slope. The hard ground made things difficult, but he was grateful to be moving and staying warm. He finally scraped out a hole and plopped into it, grateful it wasn't filled with mud.

The cold, spitting rain and wet snow he'd endured, hadn't allowed him to dry out. He was only damp and wanted to keep it that way. Stepping into a wet, muddy soup was to be avoided at all costs. Of course, if the Nips came his way, all bets were off.

He touched his ammo belt, his grenades, and his canteen, then settled into watching the light show. The occasional shot from the GIs in the canyon would bring a flurry of return fire from the Japanese. The opposite slope was a morass of darkness, but he knew 2nd Platoon was advancing toward the enemy's right flank from the northern ridge. The Japanese were giving away their positions nicely.

Ten long minutes passed before a new sound joined the

battle. Explosions rocked the canyon where the Japanese muzzle flashes were concentrated. Sergeant Mavis in the next hole over, grinned and said, "Leading with grenades…smart."

More grenades exploded with bright flashes and the canyon walls amplified the noise, making Hunter lower his head. A slight pause was followed with withering fire from the GIs across the canyon. The angle was wrong, but it felt as though 2nd Platoon was firing on Hunter's position and he hunkered even lower. A few ricochets darted overhead, but they were never in danger. The fire continued pouring into the bottom of the black canyon. It amazed Hunter that anyone could still be alive down there, but the Japanese fired back with a renewed intensity of their own.

Fire from 4th Platoon increased and for a long minute the fire was a like a constant roar. Finally, the Japanese fire diminished to just a few rifle shots. Smoke wafted up the slope and Hunter's nose crinkled, smelling the tangy sweetness of death mixed in with burnt gunpowder and sulfur.

Mavis tucked his rifle butt tightly to his cheek and barked, "Get ready. If they're coming, they're coming now."

Hunter aimed his carbine down the slope. He was on the squad's extreme right flank. He shared time between watching downslope and watching the gloom to his right. The Japanese in the canyon might've called for help. One possible route was up this slope to take the high ground. The rest of the platoon spread out to Hunter's left and faced downslope. If the Japanese came from the right, he wouldn't have much support.

He was about to bring this up to Sergeant Mavis when a carbine fired close, shifting his full attention downslope. He couldn't see more than ten yards. Someone yelled, "They're coming," and fired again. The pop of the carbine sounded pathetic after hearing the power of the earlier firefight. More pops joined in, but Hunter couldn't see any targets in his sector.

Something tugged at Hunter's subconscious. Long hours of hunting had taught him not to ignore his inner voice. He tore his eyes from downslope and gave his full attention to the right flank. He scanned and listened. The sporadic pops continued, and he heard screams and groans from wounded enemy soldiers, but he fought the urge to look.

Something caught his attention—something ill-defined—a movement. He pulled the stock closer to his cheek, but kept both eyes open, hoping his peripheral vision pinpointed whatever was out there.

He raised his voice, "Mavis—Mavis, someone's coming from the right." There was no response, so he raised his voice, "Sergeant! dammit! Over here." He remembered what Mavis had said about the grenades. Keeping his muzzle aimed with one hand, he unclipped a grenade with the other. Without taking his eyes off the darkness, he pulled the pin with his teeth. The metal was cold and left a foul taste in his mouth. He threw the grenade and it disappeared into the gloom. He spit out the pin and steadied his aim.

Sergeant Mavis finally responded, "What you…" the flash and bang of the grenade interrupted him. The flash lit up hunkered Japanese soldiers. Hunter fired into their fading impressions. He swept the carbine, firing quickly into dark and indistinct outlines.

The roar of Sergeant Mavis's Thompson firing on full automatic nearly drowned out the sergeant's roaring yell, "Japs! Right flank!"

Hunter burned through his fifteen-round magazine. Before reloading, he unclipped another grenade and hurled it into the gloom. He smacked in a fresh magazine. His grenade exploded, hurtling shapeless men sideways—some missing parts. Japanese soldiers seemed to be all around him. He fired into them methodically. More fire from his squad cut the charging soldiers down, but not before a few had lunged past Hunter's hole.

He stayed down and continued firing into legs and chests. He fired his last shot and realized he didn't have time to reload. The sickening crunch of a Japanese skull being bashed in by a vicious backstroke from Mavis's Thompson, was all the coaxing he needed.

He stood in time to parry a lunging soldier's bayoneted rifle. The soldier's forward momentum pushed him beyond Hunter, and he crashed into Sergeant Mavis's back. Hunter swung his carbine like a baseball bat and the barrel caught the Japanese soldier in the neck. The iron sights cut deeply, and he screamed in agony. Hunter lunged from his hole at the same time Mavis spun with his smoking Thompson muzzle to attack the soldier.

The big barrel loomed in Hunter's face and for a moment, he thought Mavis was going to blow his head off. He instinctively ducked and Mavis fired. The roar of the submachine gun blasted his eardrums, and he felt his face burn with gunpowder. He heard the unmistakable, meaty sound of heavy caliber bullets tearing through flesh behind him.

He landed on the enemy soldier he'd attacked. The soldier was reeling side to side, holding his seeping neck wound and screaming. His face was inches away and Hunter smelled his fish-tinged breath.

Hunter rolled away, giving himself space, then plunged the stock of his rifle into his face as hard as he could. The sound and feeling of bone shattering nauseated him, but he continued hammering until the hard bone gave way to mushy brain.

A hand gripped his shoulder and he tried to swing his carbine, but his muscles didn't want to respond. Sergeant Mavis's iron, blood dappled face was centimeters from his and he seethed, "Knock it off! It's over. He's dead."

Hunter looked wildly side to side. Bodies were strewn in

the darkness, some still quivering or trying to crawl away to die. He couldn't seem to catch his breath. He lurched off the man he'd killed and expelled what little food remained in his belly. His gut spasmed over and over, then finally released him. He rolled onto his back—exhausted—and stared into the fog and darkness.

7

Private Mankowitz trudged through knee deep drifts while wet globs of falling snow hit him in the face. He mumbled to Private Harwick trudging alongside him. "We get it coming and going."

"What?"

"This damned snow. We gotta wade through it *and* get hit in the face with it."

Harwick shrugged. "I dunno which is worse, the snow or the mud-holes in the valleys."

Mankowitz guffawed, "God knows what the stinking Japs want with this place. We should let 'em keep it."

Harwick looked abashed, "This is US territory. We can't let 'em keep it."

"Ha! You thinking of moving here? Hell, not a bad idea—I'll bet the land's dirt cheap."

Harwick shook his head. "I couldn't live in a place like this. Hell, this is the nice time of year."

Mankowitz nodded, then looked around at the surrounding peaks. Their destination was a distant peak with an unusual rock outcropping sticking out like a blood blister. It was still miles away, even though their company had been moving toward it for two solid hours. "Heard there were people living here before the Nips showed up…natives, mostly."

Harwick adjusted his rifle sling and asked, "Yeah? What happened to 'em?"

Mankowitz shrugged, "Japs shipped 'em off to work camps. Least that's what I heard. That was over a year ago now—so who knows if they're still drawing breath."

Harwick shook his head, "Can you imagine living in this hellhole then getting shipped off somewhere worse?"

Mankowitz shook his head slowly, "Might've improved their location, but not their circumstance."

"There you go again being all wordy."

Mankowitz laughed, then pointed at the rock outcropping. A dense layer of fog clung above it, making it look as though the mountain top went on forever. "Think the Japs are up there waiting for us like they were at Jarmin Pass?"

Harwick stopped and looked at the unusual outcropping. "Yeah. I reckon they are. That rock's a natural defensive point. It looks out over the next pass we gotta go through. If they've got artillery up there, they're probably getting ready to fire on us."

Mankowitz took a pull off his canteen, then blew out a slow breath. "I reckon you're right."

Charlie Company continued their march across the snow-fields for another half an hour before Lt. Callow, their new platoon leader, called a halt. Callow wasn't new to the division. They had brought him over from Hotel Company, where'd he'd been an assistant platoon leader. After a quick promotion from 2nd Lieutenant to 1st Lieutenant, he joined their platoon. Lieutenant Hubert's body had been taken off the pass and placed with the other KIAs.

As 1st Squad squatted in the snow, Private Lance gestured toward their new officer. "What you think of the new Louie, Mank?"

Mankowitz pulled his pack off and sat on it. He shrugged, "Seems like a normal guy—I guess—but we'll see what happens when the bullets fly."

"Heard he was screwing a movie star in California."

Mankowitz's face screwed up, "What—before the war or something?"

Lance shook his head, "Nah. While we were at Pendleton."

Harwick chimed in, "No way. We barely had time to shit. That's just baseless bullshit."

Lance persisted, "They're officers. They had more time than us ground pounders."

Mankowitz shook his head, "Movie stars? We weren't in Hollywood, Lance. Besides, what do you care if he did?"

Lance grinned, "I don't. Just wondering who it was? I mean, there's some fine women I'd like to bed—you know?"

Harwick guffawed, "What makes you think they wanna bed you? For crying out loud, Lance, you're not movie star material."

Lance dug into the depths of his layers and pulled out a small photograph. He gazed longingly at it, then extended it toward Harwick. He snatched it from his hand, quick as a viper. Lance lunged after it, but Harwick turned his back to him. He gave a low whistle, "Whoa, Lance. You sure you didn't pilfer this from someone else?"

Lance growled, "Read the back, asshole."

Harwick turned it over and read out loud, "To my darling soldier boy, Gary. Stay safe and come back to me. Love Dolly."

Lance lunged to get it back but Harwick passed it to Mankowitz who gave a low whistle. "I'm gonna keep this for later."

Lance seethed, "Dammit, Mank, give it here."

Numchenko snatched it away and nodded. "Wow, Lance. Nice gams on this one. Glad I've got a name to work with."

He pursed his lips to lay a kiss on the photo, "Dolly, Dolly, Dolly…"

Lance tackled the big man and they both went into the snow. Numchenko tried to keep the picture out of reach, but Lance finally snatched it back. He rolled off Numchenko, who was spitting dirty snow. Lance seethed, "You guys are assholes. I don't want anyone even thinking about her."

They all started cooing her name, "Dolly, Dolly, Dolly." Harwick was thrusting his hips suggestively.

Lance shook his head and pushed the photograph back into the folds of his clothes. "Keep dreaming, Harwick. You're too much of a runt—you've got no chance with a gal like her."

"Once she sees what matters," he winked, "She'll come running, just like your mom."

Lance's face darkened, but Sergeant Jakant shuffled out of the fog and grabbed his shoulder and held him fast. "What the hell's going on over here?" Lance tried to explain, but Jakant barked, "Shaddup! I don't give a shit. Listen up— we've got new orders."

CHARLIE COMPANY ZIGZAGGED their way up a long winding slope toward the top of yet another snowy ridge. The ugly dimple of rock, dubbed Point Able by some upper brass type, was still visible a half mile away. The ridge led directly to the nob of rock. Their mission was to make their way across the ridge and engage the defenders while I and K Company assaulted up the pass to the right.

Lieutenant Callow marched near the front where 1st Squad led the way. Mankowitz was breathing hard. The slope was steep and his legs and lungs burned with the exertion. A mix of rain and snow fell from the gray sky and the incessant fog clung to the ridges and peaks, despite the wind.

Mankowitz was impressed with their new officer's stamina. Callow walked in front of him, encouraging the others all the way. Mankowitz could barely catch his breath—let alone talk—but Callow was hardly winded at all. Staff Sergeant Calder marched in front of Callow and struggled to keep the pace.

They finally reached the top of the ridge a little past midday. Callow called a ten-minute halt and between heaving breathes, Mankowitz drank deeply from his canteen.

Second Platoon was leading Charlie Company again, facing Point Able. Lieutenant Callow straddled the knife-edged ridge with his fists against his hips, facing their objective. Point Able went in and out of view as the fog shifted back and forth. Even from this distance, they could see ugly trench scars scattered throughout the rock outcroppings.

Callow raised his voice, "That's our objective, men. The Japs are dug in and waiting for us, but that's nothing new." He gazed at the men watching him. Mankowitz thought they must look like a motley crew.

Now that he'd stopped climbing, his sweat turned to ice and he shivered. He hoped they wouldn't have to spend the night up here—there was little cover from the elements.

As though reading his mind, Callow continued, "We're exposed up here. Not only to the Nips, but the weather too. The rest of the company will be here soon, but in the meantime we'll move along this ridgeline toward the enemy. It's our job to keep them occupied so I and K Company can get past them and hit them from the flank." He lifted his chin, "We'll move along the left side of the ridge, so they won't see us coming. We'll try to get close enough to call in and adjust Third Platoon's 60mm mortars and be able to hit 'em with rifle grenades." He eyed Private Lance and PFC Chambers, First Squad's grenadiers. Lance gave him a curt nod and touched the attachment on his M1. "I want First Squad out front on this one." He eyed his radioman, standing behind him. "We only need to get close enough to call in the mortars. Don't take chances. If they see us first, we won't have much cover." There were nods all around. "Okay—move out."

Sergeant Calder bellowed, "Mank and Harwick, you're on point."

Mankowitz couldn't help seeing Lance's broad smile and Harwick flipped him the bird before turning and descending a few feet off the left side of the ridge. Mankowitz followed close behind, careful of each footfall. One bad step and he'd find himself a thousand feet downslope. The fall wouldn't kill him, but it wouldn't be a picnic and climbing back up, just might.

Harwick moved relatively fast but slowed when he encountered particularly sketchy sections. Fog swirled below them, obscuring some of the more harrowing drops.

After a half hour, Harwick stopped and crouched. Mankowitz tucked in behind him and looked over Harwick's shoulder. The slope went from a thirty-degree slope to vertical for thirty yards. The only way past it was along the top of the ridge.

Mankowitz put his hand on Harwick's shoulder, "I'll check it out."

Harwick nodded, "Be careful, Mank. I think we're close to the Nips."

Mankowitz glanced behind. The rest of the platoon was still advancing, closing the gap quickly. He turned to the ridge and climbed a few yards, being careful that his feet were well planted.

As he neared the top, the wind whipped into his face. He went to his belly and pulled himself onto the ridge top. Fog covered Point Able, but it was only two hundred yards away. The ridgeline angled down from here and offered no cover whatsoever for at least thirty yards. Beyond that, there was a depression and boulders, which would provide both excellent cover and observation. They'd also be able to continue their advance along the left edge from there. But getting past the exposed section was going to be tricky.

He carefully pushed himself off the icy ridgeline and the relief from the biting wind was instantaneous. He scurried back to the squad and was greeted by Lt. Callow and Sergeant Calder.

Callow asked, "What'd you see, soldier?"

He explained the situation and Callow motioned he should lead him back to the ridgeline. He did, and Callow quickly made a decision and relayed it to Staff Sergeant Calder who shivered beside him. "We've gotta cross that exposed section and set up in the cover beyond. It's the perfect vantage point and the Nips can't get to us."

Calder nodded but added, "Unless they've got mortars or rockets." He studied the thirty yard stretch they'd have to cross. It looked dangerous even without the prospect of nearby enemy soldiers. "We don't need to cross, we can see 'em from here, sir."

Callow furrowed his brow and pointed at the cover. "That's where we need to be, Sergeant."

Calder's jaw rippled, but he nodded. "Crossing this section's gonna be a bitch if the fog dissipates. We'll bring up the BAR crews in case we need to lay down some heat."

Callow nodded, "Good idea—the grenadiers too."

MANKOWITZ CROUCHED on the left side of the ridge. He couldn't see anything but gray sky and dirty snow. Biting wind curled and eddied from the front slope, and bits of snow and dirt tinkled off his frozen helmet. Harwick laid out on the top of the ridgeline a few feet in front of him. He was watching Point Able and would signal when the fog was thick enough to cross the exposed section.

The rest of the platoon spread out to Mankowitz's right,

staged just beneath the top of the ridge. They'd go over in squads, and 1st Squad had somehow drawn the short straw once again.

Time passed slowly and he could tell that Lt. Callow was getting anxious. Finally, Harwick's face appeared. His eyebrows were frosted white, but his eyes burned with an intensity Mankowitz hadn't seen before. He understood. If he got it wrong—if the fog lifted while they were crossing—they'd be cut to shreds. Harwick nodded and got to his feet.

Mankowitz pushed up to the ridge and was immediately assaulted by the freezing wind. Harwick was moving across the exposed, wind-ravaged ridge carefully. Mankowitz followed as fast as prudence allowed. Falling down either side would be certain death.

Mankowitz tried to keep his eyes from wandering but couldn't help glancing down the dizzying vertical walls. The wind slapped at him and he lowered himself to keep from being blown into oblivion. He felt as though he'd swallowed a swarm of bees, but he kept moving. He glanced toward Point Able and wished he hadn't. He felt unstable, and the fog was thinning.

Harwick was across, and he wedged himself into the boulders. Mankowitz hustled the last few steps and ran to his side. He felt as though his heart would burst from his chest. They exchanged quick, grateful to be alive, glances.

Mankowitz propped his M1 and aimed toward the house-sized boulders of Point Able. The fog thinned more, and he could see trenches and bunkers tucked into the rock's base. He thought he could see helmeted soldiers lined up too. He silently prayed they wouldn't see the exposed soldiers inching their way across the ridgeline.

More soldiers piled into the cover, including Sergeant Calder. The fog continued to thin. Mankowitz glanced back at the men making slow progress across the ridge and silently wished they'd hurry.

Excited Japanese voices floated on the wind. Mankowitz could see enemy soldiers pointing and turning muzzles from the valley to the ridgeline. "They've spotted us," he exclaimed with dread.

Sergeant Calder's deep voice calmed them, "Steady, steady. Don't fire until we're sure."

All of 1st Squad was across, but half of 2nd was still crossing and horribly exposed. Mankowitz watched over his rifle sights as the Japanese continued shifting. They hadn't fired, perhaps they hadn't seen them, after all. His hopes were crushed when rifle shots rang out and bullets snapped through the air.

The men on the ridge stopped and went prone. Calder cupped his hand over his mouth and yelled at them, "Keep moving! Don't stop!" He turned back to 1st squad, "Pour it on! Covering fire!"

Mankowitz steadied his sights on a soldier firing and working the bolt of his Arisaka rifle. Mankowitz fired three rounds and saw his target drop out of sight. A machine gun opened fire and the woodpecker staccato made his stomach turn. The smoke marked the muzzle, and Mankowitz adjusted his aim and fired the rest of his clip. He dropped behind cover and pulled another eight-round clip from his belt, glancing at the ridge before inserting it. Geysers of dirt and snow erupted from the ridge where men continued crossing. He watched in horror as a man lurched as though electrocuted and fell into the abyss. He didn't scream. Mankowitz hoped the bullets killed him before the fall.

The soldier directly behind him dropped and hugged the ground, forcing the men behind him to do the same. They'd be torn to shreds up there. Mankowitz rose and fired at the distant shapes, now obscured by the smoke from their weapons. The heavy sound of the BARs joined the fray, and the boulders at Point Able chipped and sparked. Explosions rocked the slope in front of the trench as rifle grenades hit their marks.

The volume of fire from the trenches and bunkers diminished and Calder yelled, "Come on! Move across!"

Mankowitz burned through another clip. It was impossible to know if he was hitting anything, but the object was to keep their heads down. He looked at the ridge. The lead GI got to his feet and shuffled his way along. Men stacked behind him and Mankowitz thought they looked like prime targets. He quickly thumbed in another clip and rose, firing. Bullets smacked the rock he hunkered behind and zinged into the air. Rock chips and dust obscured his vision. A bullet snapped past his ear and he instinctively ducked.

The tight group of GIs finally made it across and dove toward the cover. A soldier slithered into Mankowitz's feet and their eyes met. His eyes were full of fear and Mankowitz recognized Private Burke from 2nd Squad. "You alright? Are you hit?" Burke shook his head quickly and the fear subsided, as he gained control. "Get up here and help us keep their heads down."

Burke got his feet beneath him and pushed his back against the boulder. Mankowitz rose and fired into the mist and smoke. Explosions from mortars were smashing into the hillside in front of and behind the bunkers and trenches. Mankowitz couldn't see any Japanese but fired methodically until his clip pinged. The BARs continued hammering the trench-line.

Burke was still pressed against the rock when Mankowitz ducked and inserted a new clip. "Get your shit together, Burke," he yelled. Burke nodded and hyperventilated as though readying himself for a footrace. The volume of fire from Point Able increased. Burke stood, fired three shots, then crumpled. Mankowitz finished reloading and smacked Burke's shoulder. "Dammit—get in the war!" Burke's body toppled sideways, and his neck gurgled and flowed with thick steaming blood.

Mankowitz couldn't look away from his dead, staring eyes. Revulsion and self-loathing threatened to overwhelm him. Beside him, Harwick hunkered down to reload. He noticed his friend fidgeting and shaking, then saw Burke's body. "It's not your fault. Kill the fucking Japs!" Anger overwhelmed the fear and Mankowitz gritted his teeth until they ached. He stood and fired.

Enemy bullets ricocheted off rocks and sent dirty snow flying in all directions. The wind-swept Point Able and momentarily cleared out the mist and smoke. Mankowitz ignored the incoming fire and put his sights on a helmeted head. He fired twice and saw the head snap back and fall out of sight. Bullets ripped past his head and he heard screaming. His clip pinged empty, but he continued reflexively pulling the trigger.

Harwick punched his leg and pulled on his pant leg. "Reload, Mank! And quit screaming for crying out loud." Mankowitz ducked. He couldn't catch his breath and his hands shook as he fumbled for another clip. Harwick said, "Calm down. Get your shit together, Mank."

The enemy fire subsided. Harwick stood and aimed his rifle but didn't shoot. Mankowitz finally reloaded and stood on shaky legs. Even propped on the boulder, he could barely keep his muzzle steady. Thick fog again, enshrouded Point Able. Two more mortar shells exploded, the only evidence, a dull thumping.

Harwick looked back at the ridge. The flow of GIs had stopped. There was a body sprawled in the center and one GI in front, low crawling slowly toward their cover. Harwick yelled, "Get up! Nips can't see you." More GIs yelled, encouraging the hapless soldier to get off his belly and run. The GI finally got to his feet and moved the rest of the way across.

He waddled to them and slammed into the rocks, breathing hard and holding his right arm.

It was Private Ramirez from 2nd Squad. Between rasping breaths, he uttered, "Rat's gone. Rat's gone."

Mankowitz gazed at the sprawled body midway across the ridge and put a name to it; Corporal Rattinger. Despite the obvious name reference, he also had a reputation for cheating at poker, cementing the nickname.

Harwick stated, "You're hit." Ramirez nodded and continued clutching his motionless arm.

Mankowitz couldn't take his eyes off Corporal Rattinger. He thought he saw him move. "You sure about Rat? You sure he's dead?" Ramirez's eyes were turning glassy and his normally dark complexion was a pasty gray as Harwick pulled his sleeve up, exposing his blood-soaked forearm. Ramirez muttered something unintelligible.

Mankowitz didn't wait for an answer. He looked at Burke's body crumpled beside him, then glanced toward Point Able. It was still in the fog. He propped his M1 against the boulder and took off back toward the ridge.

Harwick yelled, "Where the hell are you going, Mank?"

"He's alive," he yelled. He sprinted the few yards, then slowed when he came to the narrow ridgeline. He stayed low, feeling the wind tugging at his clothes, trying to push him over the edge. Rattinger sprawled halfway across, fifteen yards away. Beyond him he could see helmeted GIs watching him from the cover of the opposite ridge.

Someone called out to him, "What's up, Mankowitz?" He thought it was Lt. Callow, but he couldn't be sure. He ignored him and kept moving steadily toward the motionless corporal. As he neared, he heard a low moan. He soothed, "I'm coming, Rattinger. I'm coming. Just hang in there."

He got to his body and got as low as possible. The ridge here was at its thinnest and most exposed. He glanced into the abyss to his right and saw shapeless blobs massed five hundred feet below—victims from his platoon. Fear momentarily gripped him. How was he going to get Rat out of there without both of them falling to their deaths?

The same voice from across the way, "I'm coming to help. Wait for me."

Two GIs were coming across and he could see the faded stripe of a lieutenant's rank on the lead soldier's helmet. "I'll be damned," he uttered. He chanced a look back at Point Able and was relieved to see it was still in the fog. One machine gun burst would kill them all.

Callow and PFC Oslo finally made it to him, and Mankowitz felt the need to salute, but suppressed the irrational thought. Callow's eyes were wide and bright. "Turn around and hunch. We'll drape him over your back."

Mankowitz nodded and carefully turned his body. Rat groaned as Callow and Oslo peeled him from the ground. "Easy does it. Easy does it," murmured Callow.

Mankowitz couldn't see their progress, but he could see the fog swirling and thinning. He could see Harwick's worried face turning from Point Able and back to the ridge over and over. He motioned them to hurry.

Finally, Mankowitz felt Rattinger's body being carefully draped over his back. He gripped the corporal's arms, securing them over his shoulders like straps on an overlarge backpack. Callow whispered, "Okay. You're good to go. Get a move on."

Mankowitz stood carefully. Rat wasn't a big man, but he was heavier than he expected. He wobbled and felt his equilibrium shifting toward the abyss. For an instant he thought they'd fall, but he got control and steadied himself. He took a deep breath and blew it out slowly, then took a shaky step.

He forced himself not to look at anything except the next footfall. He felt the fog thinning, he could imagine himself being riddled with machine gun fire and falling. His breath came in quick gasps and his legs burned with the extra weight.

It surprised him when Rattinger's dead weight was suddenly pulled from his back. Relief flooded him. He was across the ridge and Rattinger was being hauled to the safety of the rocks by three GIs. Lieutenant Callow slapped his back and pushed him toward the cover, "Good job, Mankowitz. Good job."

8

Colonel Yamasaki pulled his binoculars from his eyes and nodded to Captain Wada, standing by his side. "What are the reports?"

Captain Wada didn't need to review the document noting various units and engagements. "Our troops are holding fast and causing considerable damage to the Americans, sir. The only setback has occurred at the Pass overlooking the valley. Our men have successfully pulled back from that position as you ordered and have consolidated further west. Your plan to fortify the hilltops instead of the beach-head worked brilliantly, sir."

Colonel Yamasaki looked sideways at his second in command. "A plan you were against, Captain."

Wada lowered his head and nodded, then glared at Sergeant Ishida standing on the other side of Yamasaki, who was doing his best to pretend he hadn't heard. "True, but I see the brilliance now. The fog hides us, yet we can see them in the valleys below and engage them from afar."

Yamasaki nodded, "Unorthodox—I know—but the terrain and weather work to our advantage."

Wada smiled grimly, "Once we whittle the Americans

down enough, they'll run back to their beach-head and we can crush them with our artillery."

Yamasaki scowled. He knew his small force of 2,600 veterans wouldn't be able to keep the Americans from eventually taking Attu. Japan promised reinforcements but getting supplies to this far-off land through some of the most treacherous seas known to man, was a costly task. A few submarines had visited and offloaded supplies, but there was never enough.

He wasn't bitter about it, just realistic. He didn't suffer from delusions—he was an old hand and understood his position. The Americans far outnumbered them. They were strong, and the Imperial Japanese Navy's effort to disrupt their supplies and beachhead had failed. He would hold as long as possible and inflict as many casualties as possible, but without strong reinforcements, the Americans would take their island back.

The mention of their artillery reminded him that most of his guns were stationed near the American's northern landing zones. "How are things progressing at Holz Bay?"

The landings at Massacre Bay had been expected, but the landings to the north surprised him, and put his artillery pieces, and a good portion of his ammunition, in danger.

Wada nodded curtly. "It appears to be a two-pronged attack. The main force is attacking along the northern shore of the western arm of the bay. They are making headway, but our guns can shoot down on them with impunity and we're inflicting heavy casualties. The second force is attacking down a side canyon. They are a smaller force and, we've kept them from breaking out and joining their comrades."

Yamasaki nodded sagely. "The smaller force is a feint to keep our troops occupied and facing west away from the real threat coming from Holz Bay." Captain Wada nodded his agreement.

Yamasaki squinted and looked up at the thick cloud cover.

On and off snow showers plagued the day and would likely continue. Since landing on the island a year ago, he still wasn't completely used to the terrible climate. During the winter months, the wind could knock a man off his feet. In the early days, dozens of soldiers had succumbed to the bitter cold while on guard duty, or simply got lost and froze to death only meters from salvation. Thankfully, his men were well acclimated, and their thick, well-made winter gear was more than adequate to keep them relatively warm and dry.

"Order Captain Imai to leave a company in the canyon to contain the smaller force. I want the rest of his forces concentrating on the threat from the east. They are trying to squeeze us into the Chichagof Valley, but we must keep them from taking our artillery in Holz Bay. Without it, we will be in trouble."

Captain Wada clicked his heels and gave a slight bow, "Right away, sir." He spun and hustled along the trench leading to a well-concealed bunker. Inside, there was an immaculately maintained radio set manned by an alert soldier. Over the past year, Yamasaki insisted on digging trenches and laying communication cable throughout the region, connecting strongpoints and far-off outposts. It allowed for instant, uninterrupted communications with his commanders. He received constant updates almost as soon as events occurred and could direct his men to new threats with ease and with a full understanding of the situation.

Colonel Yamasaki watched the young officer disappear into the bunker. He sighed and shook his head, speaking low to his highest-ranking NCO. "He thinks we can win."

Sergeant Ishida, who'd been with Colonel Yamasaki since their first foray into China way back in '20, nodded sagely. "He is young, naïve, and brave. A lot like a young Lieutenant I once knew."

Yamasaki grinned, then lifted his chin and turned serious.

"I'm proud of all of them. I've never commanded better men. I only hope their lives aren't being wasted."

Ishida shook his head and his mouth turned down at the corners, accentuating his wrinkles. "They will die in battle for their homeland. A soldier cannot ask for more, sir."

"We've been through a lot, Sergeant Ishida. I'm glad you'll be by my side when it all ends."

"Begging your pardon, but your pessimism doesn't suit you, sir."

"It is not pessimism. Indeed, I'm hopeful that our sacrifice will teach the Americans a lesson they won't soon forget."

Ishida nodded his approval and looked him in the eye. "I couldn't ask for a better commander. We'll make them pay for every bloody yard."

HUNTER WAS COLDER than he ever remembered being. He'd been in countless cold weather situations in his life, but he'd always had plenty of warm clothes, food, water, and could warm up around a campfire. The clothing the Army issued was decent winter weather gear, but once it got wet, all bets were off. Without extra socks, they could never dry their feet and exposure cases mounted quickly.

He'd been more fortunate than some. He'd helped a few GIs off the exposed ridgeline. They could barely walk. When they made it to the CP, he watched the overworked medics peel their boots and socks off. Their feet were battered with trench foot and frostbite. The GIs were in agony, and the smell was enough to make his strong stomach churn. Despite the CP being out of the wind and elements, he'd left as soon as possible.

After the attack the night before, they'd retreated to their original positions. He hunkered in the same hole he'd hunkered in yesterday. Unlike yesterday, the air resupply plane couldn't find them through the dense fog and clouds. After an hour of circling, the incessant engine noises finally faded. Soon after, they got the word to go to half rations.

Hunter shivered and pulled himself into a tight ball beneath the dark green poncho. He'd been on alert for the past two hours and was glad to be relieved. He was exhausted, but the biting cold wouldn't allow him the long streaks of sleep his body craved. He slipped in and out of consciousness in frustrating starts and stops.

Someone tapped his leg and he startled. Hammond Whispered, "Hey Mack. Wake up. Come on, we've got new orders."

Hunter felt drugged. He unwound his body from the fetal position and his muscles ached. His right leg was asleep, and he pounded on it, trying to get the circulation back. It took a long time and he worried he had frostbite. Finally, he felt the pins and needles coursing down his leg and into his foot. The pain was excruciating, but he couldn't help laughing with relief.

Hammond shook his head, "What the hell's so damned funny, Mack?"

Hunter kept rubbing his leg and grimacing. "I thought I'd let it go too far. Thought I had frostbite." Hammond raised an eyebrow and Hunter explained. "Know what happens if frostbite gets too far?" Hammond shrugged and Hunter continued, "You get gangrene and they cut your damned foot off."

"You done bellyaching?" Hunter scowled at him and Hammond said, "Wilcox wants a patrol to find the Jap lines. Captain Willoughby got reports of enemy troops moving back and he wants to get an idea of what we're facing. Sergeant Mavis sent me to round up Team One. We leave in an hour, so get your shit together and don't forget to eat something."

Hunter sighed, then blew into his gloved hands. "We're on half rations. I could barely function on full rations."

"You're breaking my heart, Mack. Thought you were some kind of mountain man. What the hell's the matter with you?"

Hunter shut his eyes and pictured the raging fire his father would have going back home in Montana. It was mid-May, but Montana could hold onto winter for a long time. He shook his head, "Nothing's wrong." He raised his hands to the spitting wet snow that was putting down a fresh layer of misery. "What could be wrong?"

Hammond slapped his shoulder, "That's the spirit."

"Where'd you say you were from again, Ham? California?"

He lifted his chin proudly, "Born and raised in L.A. and proud of it."

"How're you so damned comfortable in this weather? I mean, isn't it 72 degrees and sunny every day?" Hammond grinned and looked around as though noticing the conditions for the first time. Hunter looked at him sideways, "You sure you're not from Montana—or maybe Wyoming?"

Hammond looked offended, "Hell no! I'm not a damned red-neck-hick like you. I'm a city boy." He adjusted his helmet and leaned in, "Now get off your ass and let's go kill us some Japs."

Hunter shook his head, "You make it sound like a carnival day or something." Hammond stepped back and gave him a serious look. Hunter nodded, "I'll be right there."

<hr>

THEY LEFT the relative safety of their holes and moved cautiously just below the ridgeline. An additional man, Corporal Minks from First Platoon tagged along. He replaced their sharpshooter, who'd contracted an extreme case of trench foot. Hunter admired Corporal Minks's '03 Springfield with the 2.75 power scope. Despite the harsh conditions, it looked to be in perfect condition and Minks cradled it like a newborn baby.

Hunter was on point. Since the visibility wasn't optimum, he was only a few yards in front of the next man, Sergeant Mavis. Mavis pushed him along, wanting to finish the mission before nightfall. Hunter didn't like being pushed, especially since he'd be the one to run into the Japanese first, but understood not wanting to find their way back to their lines in the dark. Getting back without being shot by a friendly was tough enough during daylight. He repeated the call sign over and over in his head, *Lilac* and the countersign, *Merry*.

Hunter had been dreading the mission, but now that his legs were moving and his blood was flowing, he was thankful. The fog was thick as ever, but there was no wind and the snow had stopped. The only sounds were their footfalls crunching through the inch-thick crust of ice covering the snow. He thought they must sound like a herd of elephants to anyone listening.

After ten minutes, Sergeant Mavis got his attention with a low whistle. Mavis pointed downslope and Hunter veered that way. He made it twenty yards when his instincts kicked in and he stopped and crouched. He couldn't see beyond the swirling fog, but he sensed something was close. Mavis scurried up beside him and gave him a questioning look. Hunter continued scanning, using all his senses.

Mavis whispered in his ear, "What is it?"

Hunter shook his head slow and whispered, "Dunno, but I think they're close."

They hunched for a full minute before a human voice drifted from the mist. It was indistinct but left little doubt. It was difficult to gauge distance, but it sounded close—too close. Hunter got the feeling if the fog cleared, they'd be seen easily.

Mavis kept his Thompson's muzzle pointed toward the

undulating voices and backed away slowly. Hunter waited a few seconds before following his assistant squad leader. As they backed away, they ran into the following GIs, and soon they were all backing away as silently as possible.

The wind came up suddenly and the fog shifted and thinned. Hunter froze, seeing a dirty streak in the snow. The voices sounded clear as the wind carried them to his straining ears. Mavis saw him freeze and he did the same.

Hunter pulled his carbine into his shoulder and made himself as small a target as possible. He desperately wanted to go prone, but the movement might draw unwanted attention.

The scene opened up as though a thick veil was being pulled from his eyes. The dirty streak was a trench-line, and it was much closer than he originally thought. It was full of helmeted Japanese soldiers. His breath came in short, shallow gasps. He settled his sights onto the nearest soldier's face. His gloved finger barely touched the trigger. The fog continued to dissipate, and he knew the soldier would notice him any second. They were close enough to see and hear individual speakers. A soldier laughed and slapped his comrade's back, as though congratulating him. What the hell were they so happy about? Didn't they know they were hopelessly outnumbered and would die soon?

The soldier filling his sights turned away from his comrades and faced directly at him. His eyes seemed to drill into him. Hunter willed himself to stay completely still. The soldier's rifle was propped in front of him. If he made a move to bring it to bear, he'd shoot him between the eyes. The distance was twenty yards—he couldn't miss. He wished he'd thought to free a grenade. He could pitch it directly into the trench and wreak havoc. But one false move and the soldier would know what he was facing. Hunter would kill him, but the others would shoot him in the back as he ran away.

The Japanese soldier continued to stare at him, as though trying to decide what he was seeing. The wind shifted, sweeping down the slope, and the fog swirled between them. The Japanese soldier leaned forward, and his hand touched his rifle. Hunter put an ounce more pressure on the trigger. The fog thickened and rolled between them again. The brief, stark clarity ended. His finger moved to the trigger guard as the trench line and the Japanese soldier disappeared in a curtain of gray.

He let out a breath he didn't realize he was holding and backed away slowly. Mavis's eyes were wide as dinner plates. He nodded at Hunter and they moved back thirty yards.

Mavis pulled them all together in a tight circle. They leaned their heads together and their breath mingled. "Holy shit, that was close," he hissed. He looked Hunter in the eye, "You two were in a damned staring contest or something. I thought you were going to shoot him for sure."

Hunter's voice felt raspy in his throat, "I—I almost did. He was reaching for his rifle. I think he thought I was a rock." The relief of still being alive overwhelmed him and he squeezed his hand into a fist, trying to keep it from shaking. The adrenaline coursing through his body needed an outlet. He suddenly felt nauseous and light-headed. He took deep breaths and blew them out slow and steady.

Corporal Minks grinned and nodded, "We should set up here. If the fog lifts again," he stroked his scoped rifle lovingly, "I could ruin their day."

Hunter looked at him as though he'd grown an ear from his forehead. The last thing he wanted to do was hang around the place. He looked at Mavis and was shocked to see he was actually considering it. Hunter exchanged nervous glances with Harwick and Hammond. They seemed as shaken as Hunter and the rest of them.

Finally, Mavis shook his head. "Our mission was to find their lines and report back." He pulled his wet sleeve from his wrist and read the time. "Let's get back to our lines. We can make it before dark."

The relief on the rest of the squad's faces was clear as they spread out in a single-file line and retraced their steps.

Minks caught up to Hunter, who was in the middle of the pack, relinquishing his point-man role to Harwick. "We could've really messed 'em up, ya know. Popped a few of their skulls and gotten back in time for supper."

Hunter shook his head. He knew Minks by sight since he was in the same Company, but he'd never had more than a passing conversation with him. "Maybe next time."

Minks nodded sagely and looked as though they had cancelled Christmas, "Yeah—next time."

9

Mankowitz counted his remaining ammunition. He had five clips for his M1 and four grenades. It was enough for now, but if 2nd Platoon was on this ridge longer than a day, they'd need a resupply or have to retreat across the ridgeline. The prospect of having to recross the exposed ridge terrified him.

The thick fog had allowed the rest of the platoon to cross with no more casualties. The rest of the company was still back there, covering Point Able from the protected ridge. There wasn't enough room for more men on this side.

There'd been a smattering of fire from the Japanese position, but nothing too intense. Lieutenant Callow ordered them to conserve ammunition and fire only if there was a high probability of a hit. There'd been a few opportunities, but the Japanese were as hunkered as the GIs.

The day was waning toward evening and Mankowitz wasn't looking forward to spending the night on this ridge. The wind was icy cold, and he had nothing except the inadequate clothes on his back. Their food and water supply was low, and sleep would be impossible.

He huddled against Harwick and Lance. Lance's voice

was strained as he shivered. "We should attack tonight and get this shit over with, one way or another."

Harwick nodded his agreement. "We'll freeze to death if we stay here and if we're gonna die, I'd rather take a few Nips with me."

Mankowitz said, "We could rejoin the company once it's dark."

Harwick looked offended, "I didn't cross that damned ridge for nothing. We're here now, I think we should roll those sons of bitches up."

Lance nodded, "I ain't going back across that…especially at night."

There was silence as they shivered against each other. Mankowitz stared at the stiffening body of Private Rattinger. "I should've taken him the other way. Could've gotten him to an aid station. Why the hell did I bring him over here?"

Harwick shook his head, "You didn't have a choice. You couldn't get him turned around and onto Callow's back. You both would have fallen. Besides, he would have died anyway. He was gut shot."

Lance added, "Yeah. He didn't have a chance. You cleared the way for the others to come across."

An M1 fired nearby and Private Montgomery cursed, "Take that, you slant-eyed little shit!" There was a flurry of return fire and the rocks chipped and the air was momentarily alive with snapping bullets. Montgomery hunkered a few yards away, laughing. He saw Mankowitz looking and called, "I got one. I'd been watching the son of a bitch and just knew he was gonna get out of his hole soon. Don't know how, just knew he would. He paid for it."

Lance nodded and called back, "One less Jap to deal with."

"Amen to that," Montgomery called back happily.

When the firing died down, Mankowitz noticed Staff Sergeant Calder making his way through the line of shivering

GIs. He wondered if Montgomery was about to get an ass chewing, but Calder briefly spoke with him and moved along until he reached their hole. "Tuck in tight. Arty's gonna lay on the heat in about ten minutes."

They nodded and Lance gave him a sideways grin, "We gonna make a move on 'em, Sergeant?"

Calder sat, tipped his steel pot back, and rubbed his forehead. "Looks that way, but not until after midnight. I and K companies are gonna move up the valley to take some heat off us." Silence followed. It was what they all hoped but also dreaded to hear. Calder got to his feet and slapped Mankowitz on the shoulder, "Good job getting Rattinger off the ridge."

Mankowitz nodded grimly and pointed at Rattinger's exposed body. There were no spare blankets to cover him, so he slowly frosted over. "Didn't do him a hell of a lot of good."

"He woulda died even if they had hit him inside a proper hospital. Gut wounds are the worst. Just be thankful we can't smell him yet." Mankowitz startled at the sheer cruelty of the statement. Calder nodded, "You cleared the path for the rest of the platoon."

Lance couldn't let it go, "Maybe you'd have liked it better if he just kicked him over the edge?"

Calder scowled darkly and shook his head slowly at Lance. "I would've done it myself if it had been you out there, Private." He turned and left them without looking back.

Mankowitz punched Lance's arm, "You should be more careful, Lance. Why goad him like that?"

"What's he gonna do way out here? Hell, I'll probably get shot on tonight's raid."

"Yeah, by him," added Harwick.

Lance looked worried, "You really think so?"

Harwick shook his head, "Nah…he wouldn't waste a bullet—more likely gut ya with that pig sticker he carries."

Right on time, the shrieking of 105mm Howitzer shells

arced overhead and slammed into Point Able. It was only 250 yards away. The ground shook and vibrated with the impacts. Waves of concussion smashed into the rocks they cowered behind, knocking dirt and snow onto their heads. The deluge of shells was intense but didn't last long.

When it was over, they shook themselves and bits of snow and dirt fell off their helmets and shoulders. "Damn, that felt close," exclaimed Lance.

Mankowitz agreed, "That's because it was." He felt the inside of his mouth with his tongue. "Feels like my damned teeth are loose."

Harwick nodded, "At least we're off to the side, otherwise a short round would've killed us all."

Lance dusted off his front side, "At least I'm not cold anymore. Feel downright cooked." He cautiously raised his helmeted head and peered into the mist and smoke. "Can't tell if it did any damage, but I doubt the Japs enjoyed themselves."

<hr>

TIME PASSED SLOWLY on the ridge. Fog shifted back and forth with the changing wind direction. Snow and sleet took turns pounding them and kept them damp and shivering. They ate what rations they had, drank water, and readied their ammunition and weapons for the coming push.

A half hour before midnight, the Japanese on Point Able shot off three parachute flares. Two floated over the valley where I and K companys were advancing. They shot the third over 2nd Platoon's heads.

Mankowitz watched the little parachute dropping slowly through the clouds and fog. It sputtered and hissed in the wet environment but put off enough light to bring the dark landscape to eery life. The woodpecker sound of a Nambu machine gun opening fire made him cringe, but it wasn't directed their way. More rifles opened fire and tracers lanced into the valley.

From their position, the bottom of the valley wasn't quite visible. "I and K must be getting hit," Mankowitz noted.

Harwick rose and risked a look at Point Able. He ducked back down quickly. "Their entire line's firing. Nothing coming this way though."

They made their way to the rallying point in the middle of their little piece of heaven, fifteen minutes before midnight. The GIs exchanged glances. Their faces were stoic and hard.

Lieutenant Callow took center stage. He pulled his non-regulation scarf off his face and addressed them. "I and K are moving up, drawing their attention. We'll stay on the left side of the ridge as long as possible. Stay out of sight even if you've got an opportunity for a shot—don't take it." He looked hard at Private Montgomery, then continued. "Scofield scouted the ridge earlier and thinks we'll be able to get within fifty yards before we'll have to expose ourselves. The grenadiers and BARs are gonna stay at that spot and cover us when we sneak on 'em. Questions?"

Answering fire from the valley rose to a crescendo. The flares extinguished, but the exchange of fire continued unabated. Staff Sergeant Calder tilted his head in that direction. "What about our guys down there? They can't tell friend from foe that far away."

"They've got orders not to shoot after 0100 hours." He gave a sideways grin, "The radio's been spotty, but I'm pretty sure they got the message." He shrugged, "We'll find out." He turned serious. "Look, we've only got enough ammo to try this once. If we fail, we'll have to go back across that damned ridge and then do it all over again. I don't know about y'all, but that scared the living hell outta me and I don't wanna do it again, so let's get this done tonight."

The GIs grinned and nodded at their new officer's candor. Mankowitz couldn't have agreed with him more. He'd rather fire his last shot and die attacking than have to cross that damned ridge again. He gulped against a dry throat and realized he'd get his chance to test that theory in just over an hour.

For once, 1st Squad wasn't leading the way. They were running tail end charlie and Mankowitz was ecstatic. The snow was only a few inches thick most of the way. Sometimes the wind stacked blowing snow into deeper sections but traversing those was much easier when there was already a nice worn track. The slope was steep, but nothing compared to the knife-edge ridges they'd already crossed. Falling here would be a considerable inconvenience but probably wouldn't kill you.

By the time they got to the jump-off point, Mankowitz was warm and relatively comfortable. It had taken 45 minutes at a leisurely pace. The shooting between the GIs in the valley and the Japanese at Point Able had dropped off to the occasional rifle shot, or a quick burst from a machine gun.

Mankowitz kept glancing back at their trail, but he wasn't too concerned about someone following them. He tucked into the hillside out of sight from Point Able, along with the rest of his squad.

The wind swirled as it crested and curled over the top of the ridge, but it lost most of its power on this side. Mankowitz thought he might be able to curl up and actually sleep. The thought made him yearn for his goose down pillow and matching comforter back in Montana. He thought about his best friend, Mack Hunter. He must be on this miserable island by now. He wondered how he was faring. He looked at the sky, hoping to glimpse the moon or a cluster of familiar stars, but the clouds were socked in tight.

The dim silhouettes of soldiers surrounded him, and he felt safe and secure in their midst, despite being a stone's throw from men who eagerly sought out his death. Word passed down for the grenadiers and BAR men to move forward. Lance glanced back at him and extended his hand. Mankowitz took it and Lance whispered, "Good luck, Mank. I'll keep their heads down for you."

Mankowitz nodded and squeezed harder, "See that you do." They released and Lance slithered his way through the shadows. Mankowitz exchanged a glance with Harwick, who looked worried. "He'll be okay," he assured him.

Harwick shook his head, "He's staying back in cover...I'm not worried about that lucky asshole."

Men in front moved up the slope toward the top of the ridge. Mankowitz followed Harwick until they were the last ones on the ridge besides the grenadiers and BAR men. The wind smacked them in the face, its power no longer muted by the ridge.

Mankowitz could hardly see the GIs crossing the exposed 50 yards toward Point Able. During their 45-minute trek, they'd lost altitude and were now below and to the left of the Japanese trenches and bunkers. He could barely make out black slithering shapes crawling up the slope. He licked his lips and pulled himself over the ridge. The first twenty feet were down, and he felt exposed. If the Japanese fired a flare now, 1st Squad would be spotted easily. Mankowitz slithered as quickly as possible but couldn't go any faster than the man in front and so on up the line. He wondered if he'd feel the bullet that was about to punch through his back.

Finally, they were on the up slope toward Point Able. Since they shared the same slope, the Japanese would have to lean way out of their holes to see them. They were closer to the enemy, but less exposed, which was a strange juxtaposition in Mankowitz's mind.

He closed his eyes tight and forced himself to get control of his growing fear. The weight of his M1 across his back was reassuring, and he concentrated on the feeling. He thought about what he'd do once the shooting started. Roll to the side, pull the rifle off his back, check the bolt and safety, and get ready to defend his life and those of his buddies.

The ground was wet, and parts were muddy from the GIs dragging themselves across. Cold seeped into Mankowitz's core, and he shivered involuntarily. He kept watching and following Harwick's worn boot soles. It was slow going. There were forty men in front of him and he thought the leading elements must be getting awfully close to the Japanese lines. An image crossed his mind of Lemmings following one another off a cliff. Was this any different? Only instead of a cliff, Japanese bullets, and grenades? *Knock it off, dammit!*

Harwick's boot sole stopped moving. Mankowitz grasped the M1 barrel sticking over his right ear and froze. The only sound was the whistling of wind through the massive boulders of Point Able. It sounded surreal and a shiver of another kind snaked up his spine.

He lifted his head and saw a quick motion from the men near the front. Tiny dark orbs sailed from their hands and disappeared into the gloom. He shut his eyes and waited. Grenades popped and exploded in quick succession like someone had lit off a brick of firecrackers.

Mankowitz pulled his rifle smoothly off his back and was aiming past Harwick in seconds. Yelling and screaming filled the night. The heavy staccato from the BARs and the thunks of rifle grenades from the ridge added to the din. GIs stood and ran forward, firing. Mankowitz noticed fixed bayonets and he panicked, realizing he'd forgotten to attach his own. He fumbled at his side, finally found it, and it clicked into place. The thought of jabbing it into another living human being—even a Jap—made his stomach somersault.

A great yell rose, and soldiers were getting to their feet and charging uphill. Mankowitz felt the surge of adrenaline and power rising in his chest. He rose with the rest of them and charged, screaming at the top of his lungs.

Dark shapes of charging GIs were all around him. Firing from the trench grew in intensity. He recognized the pings of M1 clips running dry, the hammering of Thompson submachine guns firing on full automatic, and the distinct pops of Arisaka rifles firing back.

He kept his legs churning up the slippery slope. Harwick suddenly dropped face first. Mankowitz lost his breath and went to him, fearing the worst, but Harwick was cursing and trying to get back onto his feet. "Are you hit?" Mankowitz screamed.

Harwick shook him off and shook his head. "It's slick as snot. I fell. I'm okay."

Mankowitz could breathe again as relief flooded through him. They ran side by side up the hill. They came to the lip of the trench. It was filled with GIs running and firing, some beating their rifle stocks into formless shapes beneath them. Mankowitz stepped over a prone GI lying on the lip of the trench. He reached down to help him, but when he turned him upright, he saw only a caved-in shimmering mass where his face should be. He reared back and fell down the slope a few yards before arresting his fall.

Harwick disappeared over the lip of the trench. Mankowitz got his feet beneath him and glanced behind him. He could see the occasional muzzle flare from the BARs on the ridge, but they'd clearly backed off as more and more GIs entered the trenches and blocked their fields of fire.

He dug his boots into the soft ground and forced his way back up the slope. The sounds of battle were moving away from him, and he cursed himself for letting himself get distracted from the fight.

He finally crested the trench. He stood on the bloody edge, not wanting to plunge in until he could see the bottom. He was breathing hard and fast. A motion from his left caught his attention and he turned his barrel to meet it. He could hardly believe what he was seeing.

The sight of three Japanese emerging—seemingly like magic—from the wall and charging directly at him like crazed bulls, made his bowels loosen. The leader held a pistol in one hand and a raised sword in the other.

Mankowitz didn't have time to aim. He simply pulled the trigger, firing from the hip. The swordsman staggered but kept coming and slashed the sword straight down. Mankowitz kept pulling the trigger until his clip pinged, then dove into the trench. The blade narrowly missed cleaving his head in half. It buried into the dirt and the Japanese tripped and went sprawling down the hill.

The other two were armed with rifles with gleaming bayonets attached. They followed him into the trench, but it was too narrow for both of them to attack side by side. They jostled each other, giving Mankowitz enough time to bring his rifle up. He pulled the trigger, but he'd fired his last shot into the swordsman.

The leading Japanese soldier gave him a sardonic grin and lunged his bayonet at his guts. Mankowitz instinctively batted the thrust away with his M1, but the soldier recovered and pulled his rifle back, then lunged at him again. Mankowitz went to a knee and pushed his rifle up, deflecting the thrust again. He saw his chance. He dropped his rifle and punched the surprised soldier in the crotch. The fight went out of him and he dropped his rifle. His mouth was open in a silent scream of agony. He fell sideways, clutching his ruptured gonads and vomited violently.

The second soldier was screaming and charging. He had his rifle raised over his head, ready to slash it into his face. Mankowitz had an instant to react. He threw himself out of the trench. He felt a hot pain in his side and wondered what it meant. He allowed himself to roll and roll, trying to put distance between himself and crazed soldier chasing him. He rolled up against something soft and reared back, seeing the Japanese swordsman staring at him.

He backed away on all fours in an awkward crab walk. His side ached and throbbed. He finally realized the man was immobile and covered in his own blood. He wasn't a threat. The soldier charging down the hill after him, was. He groped for a weapon, coming up empty. His knife was attached to his rifle back up at the trench.

He lunged back toward the dead swordsman and groped in the darkness. The charging soldier was closing, and his screams were threatening to drive Mankowitz crazy with fear. He finally felt what he was looking for. He grasped the smooth leather sword handle and pulled it from beneath the slain soldier's body with a sharp snick.

The charging soldier didn't slow down. He led with his bayonet and lunged it at Mankowitz' chest. It was easy to step aside and let the soldier run right past him. He felt as though he were playing tag with a group of friends on the playground in middle school.

He swept the sword across the soldier's back as he ran by and the razor-sharp blade cut through his uniform and sliced deeply into his back, changing the tone of his battle cry. He arched his back and fell, grasping at his back.

Mankowitz thought about chasing him and finishing him, but the thought of running him through was repulsive. It was dark; he was alone, and his side felt as though it was on fire.

The sounds of battle were far away. He took one last look at the writhing soldier then moved up the hill, still clutching the sword. He hoped to God he wouldn't have to use it again, but it was all he had at the moment.

He was nearly at the trench line when he heard the distinctive sound of an M1 firing close by. He dropped to his knees just beneath the lip. He got control of his breathing and called out. "I'm—I'm coming up, don't shoot."

Harwick poked his head over the side, "That you, Mank?" He stepped onto the edge and looked down at him, his smoking rifle barrel at his side. "What the hell are you doing down there?" His eyes widened, "Where the hell'd you get the sword?" Mankowitz stepped onto the ledge beside him. The soldier he'd punched in the balls had a neat hole in his forehead. Harwick explained, "Came looking for you. Found him up here clutching his balls, so I put him out of his misery." He looked at him sideways, "Was that your doing? What the hell happened to you?"

Mankowitz felt his knees weaken and he had to sit down. He felt dizzy. He shook his head, "You wouldn't believe me if I told you."

10

Another day without resupply meant the GIs of the Provisional Scout Company were even more miserable. More GIs were pulled off the line as exposure cases rose. The CP had become more of a field hospital than an HQ. Captain Willoughby ordered the soldiers near the CP to dig into the snow and the tundra beyond and they'd scraped out a relatively warm cave system. It was dark and dank, but out of the wind, snow, and rain.

After finding the Japanese line, there'd been sporadic firefights throughout the day. The GIs on the opposite ridge from Hunter's squad took the brunt of the exchanges. Japanese artillery slammed them every few hours, followed by sweeping machine gun bursts.

The sounds of battle coming from Holz Bay grew louder and closer by the hour. After a robust exchange of fire from the valley, Hunter said, "Those boys down there sound close. Just a matter of time before they sweep the Nips out of the valley."

Hammond scowled, "I sure the hell hope so. Sick of being cooped up in this damned valley."

"Bet they got truckloads of food and ammo too."

"I could go for a solid sleeping bag," muttered Hammond.

Hunter looked at him sideways, "First I've heard you complain about being cold."

Hammond looked offended, "I wasn't complaining…just be nice on some of the colder nights."

Gentry was in the next hole over. He chimed in, "Think Willoughby'll have us push or wait it out?"

Corporal Minks poked his head up. He'd stayed with the squad after the mission to find the Japanese lines, hoping to use his sharpshooter skills, but the fog foiled his efforts so far. "We should push. Whole point of being out here's to distract the Nips from the main thrust down there. Sitting on our hands just keeps us cold and weak."

Hunter exchanged annoyed glances with Hammond and Gentry. PFC Nunes, who shared his hole with Minks, piped up, "Shaddup, Minks. Nobody asked you. What the hell you still doing out here anyhow?"

Minks's voice was even and unperturbed. "Your squad's the furthest forward. Gives me the best chance for shooting."

Nunes kept his voice raised so the others could hear, "You'll just draw their fire." Minks didn't respond but climbed out of the hole and stretched as though he were back home at a local gym. "Dammit, Minks. Get down. Fog clears and the Japs'll punch your ticket."

Minks leaned down and grabbed his rifle. Without a word, he trotted down the hill toward the CP. Nunes stood in his hole and watched him until the fog swallowed him up. "He's one crazy son of a bitch. He stroked that rifle all night. Think he's got a sexual relationship going on with it."

The GIs guffawed and gave low hoots and whistles. Hammond jibed Lance. "I think he named it Dolly." Everyone laughed and Lance shook his head slowly and patted his front pocket.

Hunter said, "That guy makes me nervous."

Hammond shook his head, "Who? Minks?" Hunter

nodded and Hammond continued, "He's alright. I've known him awhile. He's a damned fine shot with that Springfield. Put up record scores on the range."

"Where you think he's off to?"

"Probably asking Willoughby to release him to go hunting."

Hunter adjusted his helmet and pulled his scarf tighter. "That's what I'm afraid of."

Captain Willoughby read the note from Lieutenant Ramsey dug in on the north ridge. Ramsey had been in radio contact with elements of the 32nd Infantry driving along the shores of Holz Bay.

Their radios had been hit and miss since leaving the Narwahl days before, but usually worked if they had a line of sight. The 32nd was close enough now that they could finally communicate. Willoughby's radios were useless in the confines of the canyon, so he relied on messengers to pass radio traffic.

His situation was desperate. They hadn't been resupplied in two days and their rations were down to dangerous levels despite the men being on half rations. More and more men were succumbing to trench foot and frostbite and his makeshift field hospital was getting crowded. The medics weren't able to do much with their limited supplies, except provide warmth and encouraging words.

After a thorough ammo and food count, he'd come to the uncomfortable conclusion that if he wasn't resupplied soon, he'd have to move his men overland to the landing beaches at Holz Bay. It would require a monumental effort which his men could have easily achieved a week ago, but in their current weakened state, might kill half of them.

The message was encouraging. The 32nd was making

good headway toward their position. They estimated they'd be at the mouth of the canyon by the next morning. The last part of the message was concerning; they were asking if they could put pressure on the enemy artillery, which was holding up their progress.

Willoughby didn't know if that was possible. Two days ago—absolutely, but now...? They were supposed to have linked up days before, but even before the operation, he'd had his doubts about the optimistic timeline. The resupply was crucial and, so far, had been wholly ineffectual. He looked at the dripping wet ceiling of the carved-out cave. Could he ask his men for one more effort?

He wrote his response on the back of the piece of paper and handed it back to the runner, a lanky kid from some town he'd never heard of in Northern California. "Take this back to Lieutenant Ramsey." The young private took it, snapped off a quick salute and took off. "Hank," Willoughby hollered.

A dirty lieutenant poked his head past the torn poncho which served as a door, "Yes, sir?"

"Get the Platoon leaders that aren't on the ridges gathered." The Lieutenant nodded but hesitated. Willoughby's voice softened, "We're gonna push this evening."

HUNTER WASN'T happy to see Corporal Minks returning to their squad, and he especially didn't like what he had to say. "I overheard Willoughby briefing the platoon leaders. We're pushing this evening." He grinned like it was the best news he'd ever heard. Hunter was shocked even more when he'd pointed directly at him, and said, "They have assigned you and Team One to me. We're going hunting."

Hunter didn't believe him at first, but Sergeant Mavis confirmed it. "I'm staying with the squad. Corporal Minks is in command of Team One for this push. Your mission is to get

Minks and his rifle close enough to their artillery to wreak some havoc. The Nips's artillery is wreaking havoc of their own on the thirty-second. You'll leave as soon as possible. Our push down the canyon will help cover your advance behind their lines." He looked each of them in the eye, "This little shindig is gonna come to an end one way or another over the next twenty-four hours. Once you're in position, do your job, then hold and wait for the calvary to show up."

Mavis and Team Two left them on the wind-scoured ridge. They looked at them as though they were already dead. When the six GIs were alone with their pseudo-team leader, all eyes turned his way.

Corporal Minks grinned, "I know this isn't what any of you wanted, but you can trust me. I'm not interested in dying any more than the next man." He adjusted his slung sniper rifle and continued, "I want Hunter on point." He pointed southwest. "Take us over those hills and down the other side. We'll avoid their lines that way and get behind 'em. Once we're past 'em, we'll know more."

Hunter gulped against a dry throat. "We'll be exposed once we're on the slope."

Minks reached down to a duffel bag at his feet. "Almost forgot. Put these on." He pulled out white smocks, painted with splotches of black and gray. "These'll help. I've gotten damned close to them using these." The GIs slipped them over their heads and pulled their filthy, wet sleeves through them. "We'll use the fog and whatever else Mother Nature provides us."

Hunter slipped the winter camouflage smock on and admired the rest of the team. They blended perfectly with their surroundings and he wondered why they hadn't handed them out to everyone. He let it go and asked instead, "How we gonna find their artillery? I mean, they don't just put that stuff out in the open."

Minks touched his ear, "Just have to let our ears guide us."

Hunter didn't like that answer, but it was as much as he was going to get. "Let's move out."

Hunter cinched up his pack. He'd filled it with the remains of his food and wrapped it in his poncho. His ammunition was spread out on his belt and various pockets. The smock covered his belt and ammo, but it was loose enough that it wouldn't hinder his access too much. He had ten magazines for his carbine and two grenades on his harness. That was the last of it, and he hoped he wouldn't need any of it, but doubted he'd get that lucky.

HUNTER MOVED QUICKLY AT FIRST, taking advantage of the fog lingering along the top of the ridge. He stayed along the ridge as long as possible. Every step took them further away from the canyon and the known Japanese lines, but toward the unknown. The 7th Recon was somewhere out here, but they had heard nothing from them in days.

Hunter finally ran out of ridgeline and was forced to move downslope. With each step, the fog thinned. He hunched and looked back toward Corporal Minks, hanging in the middle of the team. Minks motioned him forward with a slight nod.

Hunter continued down the snowy slope, making sure of each step. Soon he was out of the fog completely. The valley spread out below him and it surprised him how far from Holz Bay they'd come. The distant booms and rumbles rose from the east. More booms from the west reminded him of their goal. The Japanese artillery was somewhere up that valley, firing onto the 32nd Infantry troops.

A creek wound its way through the bottom of the valley. There were no trees to speak of, but it reminded him of countless creeks he'd fished in Montana. He wondered if there were fat trout for the taking. The thought made his stomach growl. He'd eat a hundred of them right now.

He startled when Hammond touched his shoulder and asked, "See something?"

Hunter had been so engrossed; he didn't realize he'd stopped. He shook his head, "Just trying to get the lay of the land." He looked up-slope, seeing the rest of the team watching in every direction. If he didn't know they were there, he would've been hard-pressed to see them. Their camouflage smocks fit in perfectly with the dirty-snow background.

The booming of artillery up the valley was more distinct now that they were out of the fog. He watched for the telltale puffs of smoke and muzzle flashes, but there was nothing. The sounds of battle from the direction they'd come rose in intensity. Hammond whispered, "Scout Company's pushing."

Hunter glanced back that way, knowing he wouldn't be able to see anything. A hollow pit opened up in his belly, unrelated to his hunger. "I hate that we're not with 'em."

Minks slithered his way forward, hearing the tail-end of their conversation. "What's the holdup?"

Hunter looked out over the valley, "just trying to pinpoint the artillery. Sounds like it might be beyond that hill. Maybe on the other side of it near the creek-bed."

Minks listened and watched. Another salvo from the southwest. He nodded. "I agree. We'll have to get down this slope then cross that valley to the low hills beyond." He sat and propped his rifle on his knee and glassed the area slowly through his scope. "I don't see any Japs, but you know how they are. Could be hiding anywhere."

Hunter nodded and continued his slow move downslope. He found a cut in the hill caused from spring runoff and stepped off the snow and into the small depression. It deepened every few feet and the volume of water increased as it shuttled more and more water from the high ground toward the sea. Soon the sheer canyon walls were ten feet on either side. They were well hidden and could move much quicker.

The little canyon widened as the terrain flattened and the water coursed crazily from the center, following the paths of least resistance. He'd stopped trying to keep his feet dry. It was impossible not to step into the flowing water or the many pools surrounded by mud and loamy sand.

The last time he'd had his boots off, he saw the early signs of trench foot. They looked withered and had a grayish tint. If he'd been back on Adak Island, he would've reported the finding and had it treated before it got worse, but out here—he knew he was better off than most.

He stopped at the end of the canyon and looked out over the valley. The snowline was above them about 200 yards. The valley looked like a garden of Eden compared to the ridgeline they'd been guarding for the past three days. The meandering creek coursing through the valley was more difficult to see from this low angle, but he thought he saw the far edge of it in the distance.

The rest of the team piled in around him. Minks touched his shoulder. "Good job finding that cut. Now we gotta figure a way across this valley." The tall peaks beyond the valley looked identical to the mountain they'd just come from; fog enshrouded and snowcapped. They knew the Japanese were up there somewhere, they'd seen them firing on 2nd Platoon plenty of times. "We should take these off. Our uniforms blend in better down here."

They took off the smocks and stowed them in their packs. It was only a thin layer of fabric, but Hunter loathed taking it off. The long, arduous walk had kept him warm but once he stopped, the cold would set in again. He was off the ridge and out of the snow, but even down here, the wind still had an icy bite.

Minks pointed to the low hill a half mile away. "Take us there. I'd like to get there before dark, so…"

Hunter wanted to tell him to stow it, but he nodded and moved from the protection of the little canyon and into the open. The tundra grasses were mostly knocked flat from the wind. He found thicker sections which rose to his knees and used them to his advantage. The booming of the artillery got louder the closer they got to the hill.

Return fire came ripping from Holz Bay and slammed into the mountainside across the valley. Huge chunks of tundra and snow lifted into the sky and the sound of the explosions reverberated off the mountain walls as though they were inside an echo chamber. He hadn't considered the prospect of counter-battery fire from friendly troops. He hunkered and looked worriedly at Hammond. Beyond him, he could see other teammates glancing nervously side to side. Minks scowled and motioned him to keep going. Hunter shook his head, took a deep breath, and moved toward the carnage.

The enemy artillery and the friendly artillery were dueling. Some friendly fire exploded beyond the hillock they were moving toward, well out of sight, but most splashed halfway up the mountain. It was an impressive display, but from what he could see, they were wasting ammo. The mountainside looked deserted.

He finally made it to the base of the hill and stopped. Hammond sidled up beside him and whispered, "Good job." Hunter nodded back. Another salvo of friendly fire rocked the distant mountainside. "Navy's doing a bang-up job killing grass."

"Navy?"

Hammond nodded, "Those are 5-inchers from a destroyer or more likely a cruiser. That's why they're missing so bad." Hunter looked confused and Hammond explained, "Cause they're not Army…" He lifted his hand as though to smack the side of his head, "Stupid."

Hunter grinned and nodded. Minks and the rest of the team joined them. The fading booms from the navy guns wafted on the wind. Much closer booms of outgoing enemy artillery filled the air. Minks shifted and licked his lips as though he couldn't wait to get into the action. "There might be an outpost or even artillery spotters up there, so go slow and easy."

Hunter stared at him, "What if there are?"

Minks shrugged, "We'll avoid them if at all possible. We don't wanna tip off our position or we're cooked. Move out."

Hunter gave Hammond a quick glance and he shrugged back. Hunter turned up the hill. It wasn't as steep as the mountainsides they'd been going up and down all week, nor was it snow-covered, but he felt his breath coming in labored gasps.

He pulled the wool glove off his right hand and stuffed it into his pocket. If he had to fire quickly, he wanted his trigger finger ready. When he was halfway up, he crouched and listened. If there were spotters up there, perhaps he'd hear them talking on a radio, calling in adjustments. He only heard the wind. He rose and moved forward a few yards.

It was difficult to be certain, but he thought the top of the hill was only twenty feet in front of him. He lowered himself onto his belly and looked behind him. He got Hammond's attention and signaled that he should stay put while he reconnoitered the top.

Hammond nodded, passed the signal back, and Hunter crawled forward inch by agonizing inch. It seemed to take forever, but he finally crested the hill, stopped, and listened. A salvo of enemy fire erupted. It was much louder than he expected now that the barrier of the hill was gone, and he felt a tingle of fear.

He was about to move forward to get a better view when he heard the one thing he hoped he wouldn't hear—voices. The wind was blowing from right to left and the voices came from the left. They were very close. He moved his head at a glacial pace until he could rest his right cheek on the wet grass.

Through the whipping, bending blades of tundra grass, he

saw movement. He thought his heart would burst out of his mouth. A Japanese officer was yards away, his back to him, standing tall with binoculars pointed toward the sea. If he turned, he couldn't help but see him. He was talking to another soldier to his right, hunched over a radio set. He could see the headphones over his ears.

Hunter stayed frozen in place. The wind would carry any noise he made directly to them. He prayed the others didn't blunder their way forward. He cradled his carbine in his arms in front of his face. If they heard him, he thought he'd have time to shoot at least one of them.

The artillery boomed and he took advantage of the noise. He scooted backwards as fast as he could. As the booms faded, he slowed and stopped. The wind shifted and he could hear the officer speaking and the radio operator sending the corrections.

He pushed himself further backwards. If they were talking, they wouldn't hear him. When there was only the wind whistling through the grass, he froze again.

It took ten minutes and two more salvos to get himself off the hillside. Hammond was as relieved to see him as Hunter was to be off the hill. Hammond's face lit up and he was about to speak, but clammed up, seeing the fear in Hunter's eyes and his finger placed emphatically over his lips.

Hunter pointed and mouthed the word, 'Japs.'

11

———

Hunter maneuvered Team One around the officer and his radioman. It took another hour before they were finally in a satisfactory position. They were 75 yards back from the spotters and within 150 yards of the Japanese artillery battery. Just as they'd suspected, the big guns were tucked along the edge of the hill. There were two lines of five guns. Low concrete walls protected them from the front and sides, but their backs were exposed. The front line would fire simultaneously and a few minutes later the back line would fire. Harassing friendly counter-battery fire continued, but their shots continued to be off the mark. Hunter hoped it stayed that way or their own troops might pulverize them.

Hunter lay beside Minks. They'd tucked themselves into a small band of rocks and boulders. Minks had his rifle propped between two rocks and was scanning multiple targets through his scope.

Hunter leaned in close to his ear and said, "They'll hear the shot."

Without taking his eye from the scope, Minks answered,

"You need to tell me when they're about to fire." He handed him a set of binoculars. "Take a look...see the officers and NCOs? They raise their hands, then drop them to signal fire. Their guns will drown mine out."

Hunter gulped and nodded. "Okay. How long you think before they know something's up?"

Minks shrugged, "I'm gonna take out as many officers as possible. If we're careful, they won't know where the shots are coming from, but eventually they'll sweep this ridge...it's an obvious vantage point. Leaving those spotters alive might give us more time. They won't suspect anyone's up here since their guys are still responding."

Hunter put the binoculars to his eyes and scanned the area. Neat stacks of ammunition leaned against the concrete walls. Japanese soldiers worked seamlessly bringing the shells to the loaders, while the trigger man held a lanyard of sorts. The officer held up a baton and watched the other batteries until they were all ready to fire, then the batons came down. A second later the guns boomed, and sound rolled over their position.

Hunter was nervous. He asked, "What about shooting the ammo? That'd destroy all of them at once."

Minks kept his eye on the scope. "Doesn't work like that. A Willy Pete grenade might do it, but my bullet won't." He took his eye from the scope and looked at Hunter. "Look, if we time this right, we'll be okay. The rest of the team can watch for Japs. We'll leave before they get too close." Hammond was on the other side of Minks. He lifted his head and gave Hunter a reassuring nod. Minks put his eye back to the scope. He took a deep breath and blew it out slow. "I've got my target. You tell me when to fire."

Hunter nodded. "Okay." He put the binoculars to his eyes and focused on the rear battery. The guns were loaded, and he watched the officer raise his baton, hesitate, then swing it down emphatically. Hunter waited an instant then said, "Fire."

Mink's rifle crack was loud, but it mixed perfectly with the booming artillery. Minks smoothly worked the bolt and was ready to fire before his target was on the ground.

It was the same officer Hunter had been watching. "He's down…headshot." There was no reaction from the soldiers. The officer's slumped body was behind the loaders and gunners. They continued their process without a second glance.

Hunter shifted his focus to the front batteries. The nearest officer raised his baton and slammed it down.

"Fire."

Minks fired, and an officer in the back row toppled over as though he'd tripped. Hunter saw it from the corner of his view and adjusted slightly. The body convulsed and he could see a fountain of blood covering his head. "He's down," he murmured.

The scene changed. The loading process continued, but the back row of officers noticed two of their comrades weren't up and ready. There was a noticeable delay. Hunter had his sights on the next officer in line. He held up his baton but hesitated as he looked for his comrades. Finally, he looked forward again and dropped the baton. "Fire," Hunter hissed.

Minks fired in perfect unison with the other batteries and Hunter saw the officer's head snap sideways and a red mist mixed with the thin layer of fog. The nearest two guns hadn't fired, and the soldiers were scrambling toward their fallen officers. "He's down, but they know something's up."

Minks's voice was thick and emotionless, "I see it. Keep it up."

Hunter focused on another officer in the front row. They were still oblivious. Long seconds passed and finally the officer raised his baton and thrust it down. "Fire." Hunter scanned the line and finally found Minks's target. He could just see the officer's legs; the concrete wall hid the rest of his body.

None of the rear batteries were reloading. Instead, they were scrambling to their officers and reaching for their rifles. He saw men's mouths contort as they yelled, but their voices were lost on the wind. They aimed their rifles in every direction. The front-line battery caught on and reloading and firing halted as men sought cover.

"What now?" Hunter asked.

Minks reloaded and answered. "We sit tight and see what happens." Hunter didn't like that answer. He wanted to get the hell outta there. Minks sensed his angst and explained, "They're on high alert. We try to leave cover, they'll spot us for sure."

PFC Hammond whispered, "They'll sweep this entire area soon. We need to leave."

Corporal Minks's voice was deep and full of menace, "This ain't a fucking democracy. We don't leave till I say so." No one responded.

Minks kept scanning through his scope and Hunter through the binoculars. Hunter stated, "Kicked a hornet's nest." The enemy soldiers were searching in every direction, but Hunter thought they were more focused on their hill than anywhere else.

Gentry, behind them a few yards and facing the spotter and his radioman, whispered. "The spotter's up and waving his arms."

Hunter couldn't see past the line of rocks he lay behind. Minks asked, "They coming this way?"

Gentry shook his head, "Nah. Looks like he's wondering why they stopped firing." A few seconds passed and he added, "He's on the radio now."

The wind whipped through the rocks and boulders and

made a ghostly, lonely sound. Hunter noticed soldiers being organized near the guns. They left their cover and fanned out in all directions. "They're coming this way," he seethed.

Minks's voice remained calm. "Steady. They've got a lot of ground to cover."

Minutes passed and the only sound was the wind and distant Japanese voices. Gentry's low voice, "Spotter and four others are up and coming this way."

Minks nodded, "Four? Must be his security detail."

Gentry added, "They're spreading out. Three going downhill toward the front slope. The officer and another soldier are staying on top, coming our way."

Hunter pulled his eyes from the binoculars and stared at Minks, still peering through his scope. Minks finally pulled his eye from the scope and returned his intense gaze. He looked at the rest of the team who were waiting anxiously for orders. He took another quick glance at the artillery battery in the valley below. Soldiers were moving cautiously, but the men who'd been moving their way were now diverted. He whispered, "The threat's the spotter group. Looks like the others are sweeping behind and aren't coming this way." He looked at Gentry, "You're sure there's only five of 'em? What about the radio man?"

Gentry nodded, "He's still at the radio. Six total, including him."

Minks closed his eyes for a moment. He opened them and Hunter noticed how piercingly hard they were. "We gotta take them out then get our asses back across the valley. It'll take a while for the others to crest the hill and get a bead on us." He adjusted his position, bringing his rifle barrel to bear toward the advancing artillery spotter. "I'll take out the officer. When I shoot, you guys concentrate on the others. Just a few shots, then we leave together."

Hunter readjusted and tucked the binoculars into a coat pocket. He moved to the side of a rock and sighted down his carbine. Fear rose from his gut, but he concentrated on his breathing and swallowed the acidic bile climbing up his throat.

The GIs were still as stone. The wind whipped over their backs, bending the dead tundra grass toward the advancing enemy. Hunter could see the officer and the member of his security detail advancing slow and steady. The officer held a pistol, aimed toward the sky, and the soldier swept an Arisaka rifle side to side. They were fifty yards away and closing fast. They'd walk right over their position. There was no way they wouldn't see them.

Hunter thought it would be better to kill them quietly with knives, but shunned the idea, hoping Minks didn't get the same notion. The last thing he wanted to do was kill a man with a knife. Besides—they weren't trained assassins—it wouldn't be quiet.

The screeching sound of incoming friendly artillery interrupted his thoughts. The advancing Japanese hunkered and looked over their shoulders. Minks whispered, "Get ready." The shells exploded in the valley, not far from the enemy artillery batteries. Minks fired at the same instant. Hunter barely registered that he'd fired. The officer's head snapped back, and he fell backward.

Gentry or Hammond, Hunter didn't know which, fired an instant later and the soldier beside the officer spun away screaming and clutching his shoulder. Hunter tracked him and fired twice. He thought he must've hit him, but the soldier was out of sight.

Minks hissed, "Go."

Hunter got his feet beneath him and took off, following Gentry. He glanced back and saw Hammond, Nunes, and Wilkerson high stepping after him. Minks crouched, peering over his sniper scope. He followed a second later, and they all ran headlong down the slope they'd crawled up so painstakingly slow a few hours before.

They made it to the bottom and Hunter thought they had it made when a bullet sizzled over their heads and smacked into the tundra. They kept running and another shot and another near miss made them hunker and spread out. Minks yelled, "Keep going!"

Hunter glanced back. Minks was kneeling and sighting through his scope. He fired, worked the bolt smoothly and fired again. Hunter couldn't see his target, but doubted the skilled sniper missed much.

Hunter stopped and aimed back up the slope. Minks was up and running, waving him forward. Hunter saw movement on top of the hill and fired five quick shots before Minks reached him and clutched his arm. "Move out, dammit!" he bellowed. Hunter turned and ran as fast as his legs would carry him.

They were halfway across the valley when the incoming fire from the hill increased from an occasional shot to sustained rifle fire. Bullets smacked around them and whizzed past their ears. Hunter knew he was about to die. He saw a depression in the tundra and threw himself into it. He rolled and stopped in the muddy bottom of a hole. He scrambled his way out of the muck enough to see over the lip. The others had taken cover in whatever they could find. Hunter saw soldiers streaming down the hill. Some were already in the valley giving chase, but the deadly fire was coming from the hill.

He fired until his magazine was empty, then quickly reloaded. He saw Minks tucked into the same depression. He was on his back, his sniper rifle clutched to his chest. "Minks!" he yelled. "Shoot 'em." Minks looked his way and Hunter saw pain in his contorted face. "Are you hit?" Minks didn't answer but nodded quickly. Even from ten yards Hunter could see the color draining from his face.

Hunter made a move his way, but Minks yelled at him, "Stay put. Here." He hurled the Springfield at him. It rattled and rolled within a few feet, and Hunter grasped it and checked the action. Minks' voice was strained. "I—I can't move. Something's wrong with my legs. Just put the crosshairs on 'em and…"

Hunter interrupted, "I know what to do, Minks. We'll get you outta here." He looked behind. The nearest man was Hammond. He was reloading his carbine. "Hammond!" Hammond looked up, his eyes wide. "Minks is hit. We gotta get him outta here." Hammond glanced at Minks who was staring straight up and chewing on his helmet strap.

Hunter rolled back to his belly and tucked the long rifle into his shoulder. He peered through the scope. He was momentarily confused before he realized the end of the scope was full of mud. He wiped it as best he could, then sighted through the scope.

He opened both eyes and found a soldier hunched and firing his rifle. He adjusted, closed an eye and the soldier's body filled the reticle. He'd shot many deer with a hunting rifle similar to this one, but he'd never put the crosshairs onto a human being before. It was a sobering experience. The wind was brisk from left to right, but he surmised it wouldn't have too much of an effect from this range. He moved the crosshairs slightly to adjust and pulled the trigger. The recoil took his target from view, but he quickly reacquired and saw the soldier sprawled.

He worked the bolt and found the next hunkered soldier. He touched the trigger and this time he had the stock tucked more tightly and he saw his bullet enter the soldier's chest. The Japanese fell onto his face and didn't move. Bullets ripped into the tundra in front of his face and he pushed himself backwards.

Hammond and Wilkerson were at Minks's side and were getting ready to move him. Hammond went into a crouch, offering his backside toward Minks. Wilkerson lifted Minks and he yelled but bit it off abruptly. Wilkerson draped him over Hammond's broad back. Gentry, a few yards behind Hunter, fired off a few rounds, then ducked down to reload. Bullets zipped and whacked into the tundra.

Hunter checked the breach. He was out of ammo. He yelled, "Get Minks's ammo." Minks heard him and pointed at his belt. Wilkerson flung it to Hunter. He quickly reloaded the five-round stripper clip, then hollered, "When I fire, get Minks to the next bit of cover."

Hammond glanced back but couldn't fully face him. Wilkerson called out, "Will do."

Hunter crawled his way to a position a few feet from his last spot and extended the rifle through the grasses until he could see through the scope. He scanned, searching for a good target. A Japanese soldier was on his feet and exhorting his men. He wasn't dressed as an officer but was clearly in charge. Hunter adjusted his aim to compensate for the rising wind.

The NCO was screaming orders and waving his rifle. Hunter squeezed the trigger. The soldier flinched for a second, then dropped to his belly. He'd missed. He worked the bolt quickly, noticing Hammond moving out of the corner of his eye.

The NCO was out of sight, but he fired into the area anyway, hoping to keep his head down. He worked the bolt and traversed his barrel, finding a soldier getting to his feet and aiming carefully. He had little doubt who his target was.

He didn't micro-adjust his aim, but simply pulled the trigger. The improperly seated rifle butt smacked his shoulder painfully, but he ignored it and quickly reacquired his sight picture. The soldier was down and writhing. Gentry opened fire and Hunter pushed back from the lip, leaving the rifle perched there. Hammond was staggering along with Wilkerson by his side, encouraging him to hurry.

Gentry burned through a magazine and dropped back into cover. Hunter crawled back to the rifle and peered through the scope. He saw the NCO's head poking up. He was yelling and waving his arms again. Hunter took a breath and let it out slow. He squeezed the trigger and saw the NCO's head snap back, then flop forward.

The volume of incoming enemy fire didn't abate, but Hunter got his legs beneath him and took off running. Gentry rose, fired a few shots, then ran after him. Bullets followed them.

Hammond passed Minks off to Wilkerson. Hammond was gasping for breath, but he kneeled and fired his carbine, giving Wilkerson and Minks covering fire. They descended into a slight depression. They hadn't noticed it on their journey through, but now it was like a godsend. They were out of sight from the Japanese and if they followed the natural contours, would remain so until the enemy made it to the beginning of the depression.

They ran another hundred yards. Minks was passed off to Gentry and they ran as fast as their coursing adrenaline would allow. The canyon they'd used to get down from the mountain hours before was visible, and they veered toward it.

Hunter stopped every few yards to scan their backtrack. So far, he hadn't seen more targets, but he doubted that would last. If they could get to the canyon and don their camouflage smocks before the Japanese reacquired them, they'd be difficult to spot.

They transferred Minks one last time. He was mercifully unconscious. His blood soaked the backs of the men who'd carried him. Gentry said, "We've gotta stop and get the bleeding stopped or he'll bleed out."

Hammond, now the de facto team leader, shook his head, "We'll do it at the canyon. If the Nips see us before we get there, we won't be able to shake 'em."

They finally made it to the canyon and tucked themselves into the ten-foot muddy walls. They pulled out the smocks and slipped them over their filthy uniforms. Hunter peered through the scope, traversing the valley floor slowly. He saw movement, stopped his traverse, and steadied the rifle. The Japanese were at the precipice of the slight depression. More and more appeared along the edge and hunkered, obviously searching for their prey.

Hunter hissed, "Move up the canyon. Once we're in the fog layer, we'll be invisible."

Hammond nodded and pulled on Hunter's arm, "Let's go."

Hunter shook his head, "I'll keep an eye on 'em and keep their heads down if they spot you."

Hammond considered it for a moment. He could just make out the shapes of Japanese soldiers dropping into the little depression. The Tundra didn't leave boot prints, but when they got close enough, they'd see the canyon and likely assume they were using it for their escape. "Minks will slow us down…follow us up in fifteen minutes. We'll cover you. This isn't a suicide mission."

Hunter nodded, "Okay. Fifteen minutes, I'll be right behind you."

<hr>

THE JAPANESE SPREAD out and searched the valley. A handful advanced along the depression and Hunter kept the lead man in his sights. The fifteen minutes passed slowly. He glanced up the canyon. The team was making slow but steady progress. Their camouflage was nearly perfect. He could spot them only because they were moving and only because he knew they were there. They were nearly to the base of the persistent fog layer. It was time to go.

He reluctantly turned his back on the advancing soldiers. If they saw him, the first he'd know about it would be a bullet slamming into his back. The thought sent another surge of adrenaline through him, and he had to force himself to slow down.

He stopped after twenty feet and glanced back. He was above the valley now and could clearly see six soldiers within sixty yards. They were searching the ground in front and to the sides, not willing to dash forward. He turned and took twenty more slow steps. He concentrated on each step. Slipping now would certainly give his position away.

He pulled himself around a corner and faced the valley. The enemy soldiers were close, but he'd be difficult to see tucked into the bend in the wall. He pulled back and resumed his slow, steady climb. He couldn't see the others but knew they were up there with their weapons aimed toward the enemy.

He stepped around a boulder and his right foot hung up, and he tripped. At the same instant, the whining zing of a bullet ricocheting off the boulder was followed immediately by a rifle crack from the valley. He spun and saw the deep chip the bullet had taken from the rock. If he hadn't fallen, he'd be dead.

He crab walked backwards until he was completely hidden behind the boulder. He glanced up the hill. The others hadn't opened fire. Perhaps they'd left him. He shook the ridiculous thought out of his head. Since it was only one shot and was deadly accurate, he surmised he'd been in a sniper's sights. The thought turned his guts to ice.

He took off his helmet and, holding the lip, extended it out the side. There was an immediate shot, and it ripped his helmet from his hand. It clattered and rolled past the boulder and out of sight.

This time there was answering fire from his team. The sound of small arm's fire rolling down the little canyon made him smile despite the situation. He wasn't alone out here. The rest of the Japanese—alerted to their location—opened fire. The bullets weren't aimed at him, but he could still hear their deadly buzzing as they passed overhead. He wondered if the sniper had shifted his focus upward as well.

He went to the other side of the boulder which leaned against the soft canyon wall. He scraped the mud and dirt away until he could prop the rifle between it. He slowly pushed it forward and positioned himself behind the scope, wondering if he'd see the bullet that would end his life. He swallowed his fear and scanned the valley. Targets were everywhere, but they were ordinary infantry troops, firing uphill at his comrades. He needed to find the sniper before giving his position away.

He heard Hammond yelling down to him, "Mack, are you hit? Mack!"

He tore his eye from the scope. The last thing he wanted was a squad-mate braving the fire to come for him. He yelled back, "I'm okay. Keep 'em busy. Sniper's got me pinned."

A bullet smacked the front of the boulder and ricocheted with a bizarre whining sound. He put his eye back to the scope and searched. He concentrated on the area to his right since the shooter didn't seem to see him but could definitely see the other side of the boulder. Fire from above continued but tapered off. Hunter scanned, knowing his team didn't have enough ammo to keep firing indefinitely.

He centered his sight on a clump of grass at the extreme right of his field of view. He cupped his hand and yelled, "Hey Tojo—fuck off!" This time he saw the puff of smoke and the muted muzzle flash. The bullet thumped the left side of the canyon wall. "I see you," he whispered to himself.

He concentrated on the spot, but all he could see was the rifle barrel, not the shooter. He considered firing on the gun itself, but it would be like hitting a dime-sized target at 200 yards. He wasn't a trained sniper. He'd only alert him, and he'd simply move and shoot him in the back as he tried to escape. He had to kill the sonofabitch.

He took his eyes from the scope and looked down the

canyon. A soldier was taking the first few cautious steps up the canyon. He adjusted his aim and waited for the soldier to move a few more feet. His torso came into full view and Hunter squeezed the trigger. The rifle bucked and he watched his bullet drill through the soldier's neck. The soldier staggered and blood drenched his tunic. He finally dropped like a sack of rice.

Hunter worked the bolt and adjusted the crosshairs back to the sniper's position. He saw the barrel move in his direction. His finger caressed the trigger, waiting patiently. He felt his heart trying to beat its way out of his chest. The enemy sniper knew where he was but needed to adjust his body to line up the shot.

Finally, Hunter saw his head through the grass. He wore a cloth hat instead of a helmet. The Japanese put his eye to his scope and for an instant, Hunter imagined he could see the surprise and fear on his face. He pressured the trigger and the bullet drilled through the sniper's shoulder. Hunter dropped at the same instant the enemy's weapon fired. It was well off the mark.

He smoothly worked the bolt and silently cursed his shooting skills. Was the sniper out of commission? He'd certainly hit him, but how bad? These Japanese were tough sonsofbitches, despite what they thought of them back home. If he checked, he might get drilled between the eyes.

He yelled, "I'm coming up!"

Hammond bellowed, "Covering fire!"

Hunter didn't try for stealth; he ran as fast as his aching legs would carry him. Bullets smacked all around him and he felt a tug on his trousers. He kept his legs churning as his teammates poured fire down-slope.

He finally saw them up ahead. They were tucked into a curve in the canyon, propped behind boulders and burning through precious ammo. He made one last push.

Hammond reached out for him with a broad grin on his

face. Hunter felt a hot poker in his leg and he suddenly couldn't make either of his legs work. Hammond's face changed to horror as Hunter fell hard. He rolled onto his back and stared at the darkening sky. He wished he could look upon one more clear starry night in Montana instead of this foggy grayness. Darkness closed in and he felt cold and alone.

12

Private Mankowitz remembered little after tussling with the Japanese at Point Able. Four stretcher bearers had whisked him off the hill. He'd gone in and out of consciousness as the rough trip down the mountain took its toll. They hauled him into a dank canvas tent that smelled like death. The last thing he remembered was the blood-soaked white apron the surgeon wore and his tired, light blue eyes above his surgical mask staring down at him.

The next thing he knew, he opened his eyes and saw he was in a dark tent beside other wounded GIs. He turned his head, first one way, then the other. Most of the GIs were covered in seeping bandages and were unconscious. The soldier in the next bed had his entire head wrapped in gauze. Only his mouth and nose were open to the air.

He had no idea how long he'd been out. He stared up at the dark canvas ceiling. It was rippling and snapping as the relentless wind continued its assault. He couldn't decide if it was day or night, but the wind told him he was still on Attu Island.

He closed his eyes, trying to recall how he'd gotten here. Images of screaming Japanese soldiers flashed through his mind. He cringed, remembering slicing the sword across a Japanese soldier's back. He remembered how it felt as it sliced and tore flesh and bone. He remembered watching the soldier writhe in agony, arching his back unnaturally as he tried to reach the gaping wound. He wondered if he'd survived. Was he still out there, slowly bleeding out? He hoped not. No one deserved that.

His right side ached. He lifted the sheets and saw gauze bandages wrapped around his waist. He remembered the soldier's bayonet slashing his side and awful ripping sensation. It hurt much worse now than it did when it happened.

An orderly walked by carrying a bucket overflowing with bloody bandages. Mankowitz tried to lift his head and nearly passed out from the pain. He couldn't keep himself from crying out. The orderly pivoted toward him. "You're awake. I'll fetch Doctor Bakerman. He's just finished surgery."

Mankowitz let his head fall onto the pillow. Beads of sweat dotted his forehead and his breathing was labored. His side felt as though hot knives were cutting him. He closed his eyes.

Seemingly moments later, a hand touched his shoulder and he jolted awake. Did I fall asleep? The same watery blue eyes he remembered, stared down at him. The doctor's off-white mask was pulled down, covering his chin. He had captain's bars on his floppy hat. He looked tired, but his smile was kind, and his eyes were full of concern. "How you feeling, Private?"

Mankowitz tried to speak, but his throat and mouth didn't seem to produce spit. He finally croaked, "Like I've been skewered."

The doctor smiled and checked the I.V. sticking into the crook of his elbow. "I did your surgery. Seems like ages ago. You want some water?" Mankowitz nodded and tried to sit up again but winced in pain. The doctor implored, "Don't sit up. I'll do that for you." He reached behind his head and lifted. He was surprisingly strong, firm, and careful.

He tilted a canteen onto Mankowitz's lips. It was the best tasting water he'd ever experienced, and he closed his eyes as he gulped. The doctor stopped the flow far too early. "Easy does it. Just a little bit at a time. I've got fluids going into your veins that'll keep you hydrated. Don't wanna flood you." He gently laid him back onto the pillow. "Your wound was relatively clean. The Jap that got you kept his blade sharp. It was deep and caused a lot of tissue damage, but you got off easy." He pulled back the sheet to check his handiwork. "They changed the dressing an hour ago, so I won't check it. It's gonna hurt like hell for a while. I can't give you morphine, we need it for more critical patients."

Mankowitz shook his head, "That's okay. Save it for the others, sir." He looked past the doctor at the rows of casualties. "How—how long have I been here?"

The doctor checked the clipboard and scowled. "They brought you in a week ago today."

It stunned Mankowitz. "A week? Wh—what's happening with the war...the battle I mean, sir?"

He looked bemused, "As good as can be expected I suppose. We've pushed the Japs back into the Chichagof Valley. We're closing on them from all sides. They're cut off and won't last long." He glanced at the room full of patients, "But as you can see, we're still taking a lot of casualties." He rubbed his hands together, then crossed them over his chest. "Nips don't know when to give up, I guess."

Mankowitz shook his head. "Do you know anything about my unit? Charlie Company, Second Platoon?"

He shook his head. "Nah. But you've had visitors. I suspect they were from your unit. Now that you're awake, we'll move you to more appropriate accommodations. This ward's for post-surgical and critical patients. You're gonna be fine, Private."

Mankowitz nodded and brought his hand up, intending to salute, but the captain took it, and they shook. Mankowitz looked him in the eye, "Thank you Captain…"

"Bakerman. Captain Bakerman. You're welcome. Don't do too much too soon. You'll need a few months to heal."

Mankowitz nodded, "Yes sir."

"Once we kill the rest of the Japs, we'll get you off this island." Hearing a doctor speak so wantonly of killing didn't sound right, but this was war, and he supposed the captain was as much a soldier as the rest of them.

THEY MOVED Mankowitz to a larger tent the next day. His I.V. was taken out and he took his meals sitting up even though his side still burned like fire. He wasn't fit enough to walk around, but they encouraged him to do whatever exercises he could do laying on his back. He felt as weak as a newborn puppy, but he did what he could, determined to get outta there sooner than expected.

The other patients were victims of various battles he hadn't been a part of. Some had been wounded on the first day. They were the ones limping around helping the more serious cases.

After he'd been there a day, he was sitting up on propped pillows reading the tattered remains of a Life Magazine printed months before. A filthy, short GI, and an equally filthy, lanky soldier approached the foot of his bed. "Stop pretending you can read, Mank."

Mankowitz dropped the magazine and his smile reached ear to ear. "Harwick, Lance! Holy shit, you guys look like death warmed over."

Harwick shook his head and Lance scowled, "Fuck you too, Mank. You don't look too hot yourself."

Harwick jibed, "Went to the surgical ward and when we didn't find you thought maybe you died…but no such luck."

Mankowitz laughed and his side sent needles of pain. "Don't—don't make me laugh."

"How you feeling?" asked Lance.

He shrugged, "Fine, I guess. Doc says he expects a full recovery." They both nodded and Mankowitz asked, "So tell me what's been going on. I don't know what the hell's happening out there."

Harwick's face darkened. "Well, we took Point Able the day you got wounded. There were a few more bunkers and trenches up the hill. Us and K company closed on 'em from two sides. They didn't last long." He shook his head and stared at his hands. "We lost Monty. Jap was playing possum and when he turned him over, he touched off a grenade. Killed 'em both."

"Jesus, Joseph, and Mary," Mankowitz sighed.

Lance added, "They pulled us off the line for a few days after that. We visited you, but you were out cold." His face darkened too, "We just got done helping out with The Nose."

"The Nose? What the hell's that?"

"Piece of land sticking out into the valley. Japs were thick as thieves in there. Bombed the crap outta them, but the only way to get 'em out was one by one. The Seventeenth got the brunt of things—lost a lot of men. They called us in to help clean up the pockets."

Harwick nodded somberly. "Now we got 'em pinned into the Chichicoo, or whatever the hell they call it."

"Chichagof," corrected Lance.

"Yeah, that's it. The troops they landed near Holz Bay hooked up with the Provisional Scout Company and took the rest of the Jap artillery, then pushed 'em over the hill and met up with the rest of us. Japs got the sea to their backs and they're surrounded on every side." He blew out a long breath, "Won't be long now."

Lance nodded, "Of course the stupid sons of bitches won't surrender. We'll have to kill every last one of 'em."

"I've got a buddy in that Scout Company. Heard anything else about them?"

Harwick shrugged, "Heard they had a hard time of it, but that's nothing new."

Lance chimed in, "I saw some of 'em. Lot of walking wounded. I heard they ran out of food and didn't eat for three days."

A soldier limping past heard the tail-end of the exchange and stopped. "You heard right. Damned fog kept the resupply planes from finding us. But we got through it alright —for the most part."

Lance puffed out his chest, "Mind your own business, why don't you."

The soldier puffed his chest but before either of them could escalate things, Mankowitz asked, "You know a guy named Mack Hunter?"

The soldier's glare faded, and he smiled, "Sure I do. Mack's in my unit." He pointed, "In fact, he's right over there."

Mankowitz turned too quickly and winced in pain but swallowed his yelp. A cold sweat beaded on his forehead. "He's here? Is—is he alright?"

The soldier looked alarmed, seeing Mankowitz's face turn white. "A hell of a lot better than you look." He grinned, "I'll bring him over, you rest easy."

They watched him go to the other side of the sprawling tent, weaving his way through rows upon rows of cots. Harwick shook his head. "What're the chances of that?" he wondered.

"I knew he was on the island…least I figured he was. Their troop ship split off from us, but…" he shrugged, "Well, I just had a feeling he was here too."

The soldier led a solid-looking man sporting crutches

along the lanes of wounded. Mankowitz's smile broadened as he recognized his old buddy. "Mack!" he hollered.

The soldier on crutches pulled up short and he smiled and shook his head in wonder. "Mank? Is that you?"

Mankowitz spouted, "In the flesh!"

Lance and Harwick parted and Hunter nearly fell over himself getting to the bedside. He leaned down and hugged Mankowitz, who grimaced in pain, but didn't want to let go. Hunter pulled back, "Oh sorry. You're wounded."

Mankowitz nodded, "Yeah, my right side." He looked his old friend up and down. "You too? They shoot you in your big ass?"

"No, you son of a bitch. They got my leg. Sniper." He looked Mankowitz up and down, "How'd you get it?"

The thought made him cringe. "Bayonet. Son of a bitch skewered me."

Harwick nodded and added, "That was right before Mank gave him the samurai sword treatment." He chopped his hand, mimicking the move.

Hunter looked from Harwick, then back to Mankowitz in disbelief. "That true?" Mankowitz's face reddened and he shrugged. Hunter shook his head slow, "I wanna hear all about that."

Lance stepped forward, "By the way—I stowed that thing with your stuff. I told the orderlies if it wasn't there when you got outta here, there'd be hell to pay."

Mankowitz wasn't sure how he felt about that. The sword was war booty, but it would also remind him of that fateful day every time he looked at it. "Thanks, Gary."

Introductions were made all around and they jawed and joked until the orderlies had to escort the visitors out and force the patients back into their beds.

Hunter woke in a cold sweat and for an instant, thought he was back in the canyon being hunted by the Japanese sniper. In this rendition, he couldn't move, and the sniper's shots got closer and closer.

He shook himself the rest of the way awake. He took deep breaths, in and out slowly, until the harrowing nightmare slowly faded. He was tired but feared falling back into the dream. The single light gave the inside of the tent a soft glow. He wondered what time it was and figured it had to be near dawn. No sense trying to sleep, it's all he'd been doing since he arrived a week and a half ago.

He found his crutches and made his way past the aisles of cots and snoring GIs. There was the occasional terrified cry as nightmares assaulted minds here and there. He wondered how long his own nightmares would last. He'd started having them a few days after his friend Mankowitz arrived a week ago.

They'd spent every moment together since finding one another. He hadn't known he'd been worried about him, but when he saw him safe, an invisible weight lifted from his shoulders.

They'd spent the next several days talking about home. Each shared their own war-stories but once they were told, they didn't revisit them. Talking about home and past shared experiences made them forget the war raging just a few miles out the front tent flap—at least for a little while.

The wind continued to carry the distant thumps of artillery and warfare to their ears. They craved information. The news was mostly good. The Japanese position was slowly being chipped away—bit by bit. No one expected them to last more than a few days at the most.

Hunter found Mankowitz's rack and looked down on his friend. Mankowitz sensed his presence and opened his bleary eyes. He sat up slowly until he was propped on his elbows. His wound still ached, but nothing like when he'd first arrived. It felt more like a side-ache he used to get when he ran too hard. He'd been walking the floor with Hunter for days now and felt himself improving. "Can't sleep?" he asked.

Hunter nodded, "Nearly dawn anyway. Wanna do a lap or two before breakfast?"

Mankowitz nodded and pulled the wool blanket off his legs and gingerly swung them over the side. He waited and was happy to note that he didn't feel dizzy. He got to his feet and touched his side. There was still a dressing over the wound, but it was there to keep the stitches from being pulled inadvertently. He resisted the urge to scratch.

Hunter leaned the crutches on the cot. "Think I'll try it without them this time."

Mankowitz nodded. Hunter had always been an over-achiever. It was why he was drawn to the Scout Company in the first place—the challenge. Why would healing be any different for him?

The first lap was slow, mostly because it wasn't well lit but also because they were still stiff from sleeping. The second lap was faster and by the time they were on their third, the sun was up, and other patients were stirring.

Hunter said, "Feel so naked without my carbine."

Mankowitz nodded his understanding. "I know. I asked if I could keep my rifle at my bed, but they refused. Too many nightmares. They think someone might accidentally shoot. It's like we're in the loony bin or something."

Hunter nodded but didn't mention his own nightmares. He was sure it was temporary and would fade with time. "I asked Gentry to find where they're keeping our stuff, just in case. He said they're stacked across the street near an ammo dump."

Mankowitz guffawed, "They've got the ammo dump next to the hospital? What if the Japs drop an artillery shell on it?"

Hunter shrugged, "We wouldn't know about it if they did, just be dust in the wind."

Mankowitz shook his head woefully, "Army logic."

"Don't worry; most of the Jap arty got taken out by our guys in Holz Bay."

Mankowitz shuffled around a cot with a snoring GI on it. "I know, but how much thought went into that decision?"

Hunter grinned, "Not much. But don't forget, this is the same Army that thought we'd take this turd island in three days. We're coming up on three *weeks*."

Mankowitz stopped in his tracks. "Holy shit, you're right. It's May 27th. Seems like we landed ages ago."

13

———

Colonel Yamasaki and his remaining men were cornered, and trapped in Chichagof Valley. Despite their dire situation, the troops were in high spirits. Very few officers had survived and losing them caused Yamasaki pain, but also ebullient pride in their sacrifice to the Emperor.

Captain Wada stood by his side inside the fortified bunker near the town of Attu. The few villagers that lived there had long since been sent to Japan where they would labor and help in the effort to unite Asia. They'd been a pathetic bunch, but he respected their tenacity for carving out an existence on these miserable shores.

The snow-covered mountains surrounding them used to be manned by his men but were now held by the Americans. They could fire on them at will and often did so at all hours of the day. It was only a matter of time before the Imperialists made the final push. He had no intention of sitting here waiting to die.

He smacked his gloves against his leg. "We have three choices. Stand and fight, melt away into the mountains and fight them as guerrillas, or counterattack."

Captain Wada nodded his agreement. "All are honorable choices, sir." He was sure Yamasaki had already made his choice, so he didn't voice his own opinion. If Colonel Yamasaki wanted his opinion, he'd ask for it.

Yamasaki raised his chin and clasped his hands behind his back. "I have sent a message telling command of my decision to counterattack. I did not wait for a reply but know they will approve. The Americans are overconfident. We shall thrust straight up the valley, cross into Massacre Bay and and seize their artillery batteries. We will fire on them with their own ammunition and destroy them. They will be in disarray and will need to retreat and re-consolidate their forces."

Captain Wada nodded his approval. "They are strong on the ridges, but thin in the center. A fine plan, Colonel. We have been fighting them from entrenched positions, they won't expect a frontal attack."

Yamasaki knew the plan had little hope of success, but he exuded confidence. "Gather the men. Be sure they get full rations and bring out the remaining Sake. We attack at 0300 tomorrow. I will personally lead the attack."

Captain Wada bowed, "Sir, it would be an honor to be by your side."

Yamasaki nodded, "We will divide our men between us. You will lead the Northern group and I shall lead the Southern group. Have the men assembled at 0200 hours. I will give them their orders and toast their success."

COLONEL YAMASAKI COULDN'T HELP SMILING. His men were raucous and obviously enjoying themselves. He only wished he could make their night better by providing female companionship. But none of them had seen a female since leaving Japan.

Since the Americans landed nearly three weeks ago, his

men had been fighting and dying every day. He was proud of all of them. They'd fought like tigers, only giving ground when it was necessary and doling out death and destruction for every meter they lost. He checked his watch, 0100; it was time to visit the infirmary.

The night was unusually clear. The ever-present wind was there, but the fog, spitting rain, and snow had abated. Good weather for an attack. The gods were smiling upon him.

He stepped into the low light of the transformed schoolhouse. It was jammed full of wounded soldiers. The smell of putrefaction and death assailed him, but he was used to it by now. He'd first smelled it in China. It seemed ages ago now. He glanced at Sergeant Ishida. He'd been by his side then, as he was now.

The harried doctor Sano shuffled over and snapped off a crisp salute. "Major Sano at your service, Colonel."

Yamasaki knew all of his officers quite well. Major Sano had gone to medical school in California and spoke perfect English. He'd returned to Japan a few months before ill will between the two nations exploded into war. He was a good man and an even better doctor. He'd kept soldiers alive, despite being low on every kind of medication. As far as Yamasaki knew, the man never slept.

Wounded soldiers tried to sit up as he entered, but he waved them back, "At ease. As you were." He pulled Sano aside, "As I'm sure you heard, I will lead a counter-attack in a few hours."

Major Sano nodded, "Yes, sir. I heard the news. What do you need from me?"

"We will kill many Americans today, and many of us will die honorably. Every man that can walk will need to fight. Unless we achieve total victory, those that can stand, should stay here, and help the critical cases honor their ancestors by taking their lives. You will do the same, doctor. It is your duty to make sure those that can't end their lives are helped into the afterlife."

Major Sano bowed deeply, "The walking wounded are already with the others. No one left here will be dishonored, sir."

Yamasaki put his hand on the young doctor's shoulder. "I know this is difficult for you. You're a healer. Your Hippocratic oath means nothing in our culture. You understand that," he stated flatly.

Major Sano nodded, "Of course, sir. I will do my duty." He lifted his chin, "It was an honor to serve with you, Colonel Yamasaki."

Yamasaki squeezed his shoulder and nodded, "The honor was all mine, Major Sano."

Yamasaki sauntered through the wounded soldiers and said a few words of encouragement to each of them. By the time he left, his eyes sparkled with pride and sorrow. Once outside, he stopped and looked at the skittering clouds. He faltered for a moment, as though unsteady, and Sergeant Ishida put a hand on his old friend's shoulder.

Yamasaki patted his hand, "Emotion overwhelms me. Such fine soldiers." He lifted his chin and steeled his soul. "It is time to address the rest of the men."

As they neared the center of the camp, the unmistakable sounds of partying soldiers reached him. There wasn't enough Sake to get the men drunk, just enough to give them courage. Flares sparked in the distance, marking the front lines. A company of soldiers stood ready to repulse the Americans if they came now. They'd been rotated forward and replaced by another company, so no one was left out of the extra rations and alcohol.

The room quieted when Yamasaki entered. The soldier's faced him and braced with pride. Yamasaki raised his voice. "Today, we honor our Emperor. Today, our ancestors will look down upon us and see the true fighting spirit of the soldiers of the rising sun. Today, we embrace our destiny. Today, we honor our families." He paused and bellowed louder, "Today, we crush the American devils!" A raucous cheer went up. Yamasaki unsheathed his Samurai sword. It had been in his family for generations. He held it stiffly to his shoulder then raised it quickly and the soldiers joined his yell with each raising and lowering, "Banzai!—Banzai! —Banzai!"

"WHAT THE HELL are they so happy about?" asked Sergeant McMurtry. He'd just joined the two GIs at the forward outpost.

Private Vasquez and PFC Brown were to either side of him, hunched low and out of the wind. Vasquez shrugged, "One last party? They've been going at it all damned night."

The forward OP was on the northwest side of Lake Cories, facing the hopelessly surrounded remnants of the Japanese. The wind coming off the lake had an extra bite to it, but the fog had lifted, and the mixed rain and snow had stopped for a welcome change.

Sergeant McMurtry shrugged, "It does sound like a party, doesn't it?"

PFC Brown sighed, "How long we have to stay out here, Sergeant?"

"You know as well as I do. You'll be relieved at dawn."

Vasquez shook his head, "How'd we get the short end of the stick? Half the division got sent off the line and here we sit."

McMurtry gave him an evil grin, "Guess you're just special Vasquez." He checked the radio, "This thing seems to work tonight. Keep checking in on the hour."

PFC Brown nodded, "Yes, Sergeant." A friendly flare erupted overhead, and they hunkered to keep out of its eery light. The scene in front of them looked the same as it always did; bleak and cold.

McMurtry waited for the flare to hiss into the ground and extinguish. "Stay on your toes and report anything strange."

They both nodded and chimed, "Yes, Sergeant."

McMurtry left, leaving them watching the dark night. The enemy soldier's voices wafted over them in waves depending on the wind. With two hours until dawn, the partying seemed to stop. They strained but couldn't hear the raucous laughter anymore. The only sound was the wind-driven waves lapping the shores of Lake Cories.

Brown pulled his scarf tighter, "Finally. They're all partied out."

Vasquez nodded, "Be a good time for us to attack. They're probably all drunk and passed out."

Brown shook his head, "That's not gonna happen. Everyone's back getting hot chow and a nice warm rack."

"Yeah, everyone but us," complained Vasquez.

Fifteen minutes passed. They hunkered lower. They were still twenty minutes from the top of the hour, when they'd call in their radio check. They both perked up, hearing loud cheering. It was followed closely with a loud call of 'Banzai.'

They exchanged glances. Vasquez asked, "Banzai? What the hell does that mean?"

Brown shrugged, "Just Jap gibberish."

"Should we call it in?"

Brown checked his watch. "We'll mention it when we check in. I don't wanna call in twice."

Five minutes before 0300 hours, they heard the Banzai call again, but this time it was much closer and seemed spread across the entire valley. Instead of fading away like last time, the Japanese voices continued, unabated.

They exchanged worried glances. PFC Brown grasped the radio handset. "I'll call it in. Fire a flare."

Vasquez nodded and clambered to find the flare gun in the

dark hole. He finally found it, loaded it, and fired. The bright white incandescent light arced overhead gracefully and lit up the tundra. At first, nothing looked out of the ordinary. Then they saw undulating movement. It appeared as though they were being charged by a herd of deer, or elk, but there were no deer or elk on this island.

"Oh my God," uttered Vasquez. "It's the whole Jap Army!" He picked up his M1. "We gotta get outta here! Now!"

Brown was on the radio yelling, "Come in! Come in! Are you receiving? The whole Jap Army's coming. We need artillery! We need support!"

A tired voice answered, "Calm down. What did you say? Repeat your message."

Vasquez fired his M1 into the charging mass until his clip pinged. He fumbled to reload, but the wave of screaming Japanese soldiers cut him down with multiple rifle shots. Brown, still hunkered, felt warm blood splatter his face and hand. He saw Vasquez drop and looked up in time to see a looming silhouette slashing down at him with a fixed bayonet. The radio handset fell from his hand and the tinny, bored voice continued asking for a sitrep.

BREAKING out of Chichagof Valley was exhilarating. It surprised Colonel Yamasaki how easily his charging men rolled through the American defenses. The enemy was caught completely by surprise. The first real resistance they faced was once they were well past Lake Cories.

His men gleefully charged through stunned pockets of American soldiers and either shot, grenaded, or bayoneted them. Their swift, unrelenting charge through the early morning darkness didn't falter for the first few hours and

Yamasaki thought his plan to push straight through to Massacre Bay, might actually work.

His men destroyed soldiers, equipment, and even a large ammunition dump. The explosion lit up the darkness and he could see the pass they'd need to go over. Once beyond it, they'd have a clear path to the enemy artillery batteries.

The darkness was lifting, and the day promised to be gray. He kept his sword out and pushed his men forward with gleeful battle cries. Fifty yards ahead, a line of enemy soldiers dropped to their bellies and opened fire. Beyond them, a small city of tents flapped in the wind.

His men crumpled as bullets sliced into them, but the others kept up their frantic pace and soon closed the distance.

Yamasaki ran forward faster than his sixty-year-old legs had carried him in years. He felt like a god surrounded by demi-gods. He ran with his sword in his right hand and his service pistol in his left.

His men fell upon the line of enemy soldiers and chaos ensued. Men slashed and clawed at one another in brutal hand to hand combat. He reached the line and focused on an American sergeant. He was driving his bayonet into one of his men. The Japanese soldier arched his back and screamed. The American pulled his bayonet and spit onto the dying man's back. Anger filled Yamasaki like dragon fire, and he charged, screaming and waving his ancient sword.

The American sergeant looked up, but not in time to defend himself. Yamasaki sliced sideways and his blade cut through the soldier's neck, barely slowing its bloody arc. The sergeant's head spun loose and fell beside his feet. An explosion of blood spouted from the cleanly cut neck and the soldier's torso swayed but didn't topple.

Yamasaki ran past and fired into the back of another soldier grappling with one of his men. His man pushed the stricken American off and drove his bayonet into his stomach with a vicious jab. Yamasaki saw he was using a long stick with the bayonet lashed to the tip. His men were low on supplies and resorted to any weapons they could find or fashion.

The soldier snatched the American's M1 and slung his ammo pouch over his shoulders like a bandolier. He grinned at Yamasaki and they continued charging through the doomed American camp.

Soldiers fired through the flimsy canvas tents and threw grenades inside. The explosions distended the fabric, reminding Yamasaki of a Puffer fish. Stunned, bloody soldiers staggered from the front flaps. They were shot and run through with bayonets.

He saw Americans running away in all directions. Those that stood to fight, died. His men fired and gave chase, but Yamasaki kept control and bellowed for them to return. Their objective was the pass and Massacre Bay beyond. His men complied immediately, despite their overflowing bloodlust, and soon they were beyond the destroyed camp.

Yamasaki kept his eyes on a low hill ahead. It appeared to be full of equipment. He wondered if perhaps it was another ammunition dump. Perhaps it was a forward artillery battery. Regardless, he could see many enemy soldiers darting this way and that among the equipment and tents. He calmed his mind and thought tactically. If he steered his men past it, the Americans could fire on them as they passed. He didn't know what was up there, but even one well-placed machine gun nest would decimate, or more likely halt, their advance.

He yelled, "Sergeant Ishida!"

The NCO was only yards behind. He ran up beside him, "Here, sir."

Yamasaki pointed his bloody sword at the low hill. "We must take that position. Once we do, we'll have an open path to Massacre Bay."

The old sergeant saw the truth of it immediately. Between

puffs of breathing, he said, "Yes, sir. We'll take it quickly. Probably rear echelon soldiers, sir."

Yamasaki nodded. "Yes," he agreed. He pointed, "Captain Wada is that way. Send a few men to relay the message." Ishida nodded and relayed the message to nearby troops. They sprinted to pass the message as though hell hounds pursued them.

Yamasaki pointed his sword at the new objective and yelled, "Attack that hill!" He didn't know exactly how many soldiers he had left. He'd lost many already this morning, but not nearly as many as the enemy. Some hadn't been able to keep up with the frenzied pace, and some had gotten mired down in brutal engagements. His men were spread out from here all the way back to Chichagof, but his main force still numbered over a thousand men. They'd simply overwhelm the hapless soldiers.

They moved like an inexorable tide toward the base of the hill. When they were half a kilometer from the base, a machine gun opened fire. Bullets stitched through the first line of soldiers and they stumbled and fell. The survivors jumped and weaved over them and kept moving steadily.

Rifle fire added to the machine gunfire and more men fell. Some soldiers paused, raised their rifles, and fired before continuing their charge. Their yells echoed from the walls of the valley, mixing with sound of gunfire.

By the time they made it to the base of the hill, many soldiers were out of the fight. Yamasaki raised his sword. "Banzai!" He yelled. The battle cry rose through the ranks, bringing the men into a renewed frenzy. Yamasaki ran with them, weaving through dead or dying soldiers. Another machine gun opened fire from the American right flank and swept them. Men fell, but the overall push continued.

The top of the hill bristled with rifles and was obscured with clouds of gun smoke. Bullets whizzed past Yamasaki and he wondered how he was still alive. His men were encouraged by his presence. They saw him charging and fighting fearlessly beside them. They charged with renewed vigor.

Soldiers near the front hurled grenades. They didn't wait for their detonations, but followed their throws, unafraid to die from their own blasts. The explosions rocked the American lines and Yamasaki thought the support troops would break and run, but instead they closed ranks and continued killing his men with concentrated, accurate fire. Hundreds had fallen, but they were near the top.

The ground shook with explosions and soldiers were lifted and ripped apart as mortar shells rained down upon them. Yamasaki dug his boots into the soft tundra, willing his legs to keep churning, despite the burn. Soldiers bypassed him and he wished he were a younger man.

The soldier directly in front of him was suddenly thrown backwards. His torn body stopped most of the mortar shell's steel fragments, but his body had slammed into Yamasaki and sent him reeling backwards. He felt a dull ache in his side.

For a moment, his mind shunted away from the battlefield. He stared at the sky. Thick gray clouds moved as though he were gazing into a witches' cauldron. It felt good to lay there. Calm. He'd be happy to die here.

He felt hands upon him and through his ringing ears, he heard Sergeant Ishida's desperate voice. "Colonel Yamasaki!"

Yamasaki returned to the battlefield and shook his head. He struggled to his feet, feeling the deep ache in his side. He glanced down and saw the right side of his body glistening with blood. He knew he was beyond help, but he shook Ishida off and lifted his sword with shaking arms.

Soldiers still charged, but the mortars had torn large swaths of destruction through their ranks. They faltered, seeing their commander struck down. He reached to the depths of his soul and yelled one last time, "Banzai!"

He lunged forward and his men rallied and charged with

renewed vigor. They crested the hill, and his men were finally among the desperate Americans. They slashed, grappled, and died.

Yamasaki swung his sword, catching a soldier's arm. The soldier dropped his rifle, screamed, and clutched his nearly severed arm. Yamasaki ran him through, and their eyes met. The soldier was young, and his eyes were pleading and full of pain. Yamasaki pulled his sword and stepped past the dying soldier.

His men slashed and hacked and were finally beyond the first line of defense. Yamasaki felt weak with blood loss, but he was ecstatic. They were going to do it. The way to Massacre Bay was open. He limped after his men as they swarmed into the base.

Multiple machine guns opened fire all at once. The heavy concentration of lead shredded his men. It infuriated him. They mowed them down as though they were mere strands of wheat.

Sergeant Ishida yelled and ran in front of Yamasaki. The colonel watched in detached horror as his best and oldest friend's body writhed and shook with .30 caliber bullet impacts.

Yamasaki raised his sword and lunged past Ishida's body. The nearest enemy machine gun muzzle was only meters away. The red-hot barrel smoked and hissed. The assistant gunner was struggling to reload. Yamasaki used the last reserve of energy he could muster and charged.

He took the last few steps and raised his sword to sweep it across the gunner, but the machine gun opened fire and it cut Colonel Yamasaki in half.

14

Hours Earlier

Another nightmare awakened Hunter. Like most mornings when there were only a few hours until dawn, he took the time to walk. Mankowitz was sound asleep, so he didn't bother him. The night wasn't as miserable as usual, so he ventured outside the tent and walked the perimeter.

He stepped carefully, not wanting to step into a hole and reinjure his leg. He had his crutches in case he got himself into trouble. A few bored sentries smoked cigarettes along the perimeter. They nodded at him as he limped past.

The glow of flares toward the front lines a few miles away reminded him of the still unfinished work that needed to be done. He knew he wouldn't be a part of it. He wondered what it must be like for the Japanese soldiers out there; cut off and hopeless. He'd heard stories from other GIs about Japanese soldiers killing themselves with grenades rather than surrendering. He didn't understand their way of thinking, but he couldn't help but admire their fighting spirit.

He pulled up short and stopped, listening. The last few nights had been quiet, but now he heard distant explosions and gunfire. The sounds of battle increased until it was nearly constant. He wasn't privy to command decisions, but scuttlebutt was as reliable as though it had come straight from Captain Willoughby's mouth. He had heard nothing about a push this morning.

The intensity diminished considerably, but the shots and explosions he heard sounded closer. He retraced his steps and approached a sentry. He had his rifle off his shoulder and the discarded cigarette smoked on the ground near his boots. "What the hell's going on down there?"

The GI turned slightly and shrugged. "Dunno. Sounds like it's getting closer. Better get back inside, soldier."

Hunter bristled at being treated like he needed protection. He didn't move. A bright explosion erupted in the valley. Flames roiled skyward and a sustained rumble grew until it made Hunter's sinuses ache. "What the hell just blew up?"

The GI looked annoyed but answered, "Think that's the ammo depot. Someone must've gotten too close with a cigarette or something."

Hunter guffawed, "With all that shooting beforehand?" He shook his head, "Something's up."

The sentry still looked skeptical. "If something was up, they'd tell us."

"Not if the Nips are attacking. They don't put out flyers, far as I know."

The GI scowled, "Get back inside. If something's up, we'll get orders."

Hunter scowled but turned and left. Instead of going back to the infirmary, he took a detour across the street. He dropped the crutches, grabbed two M1s, pouches of ammo, and all the grenades he could carry.

The infirmary was buzzing. The immense explosion was impossible to sleep through. Wounded soldiers listened to the sounds of battle and discussed what it might mean.

Hunter went straight to Mankowitz's rack. He was lacing up his boots. Corporal Minks was beside him, holding his service .45. Minks still looked pale, but the determination in his hard, blue eyes left no doubt; he would not take whatever was coming sitting down.

Mankowitz took the offered M1, loaded it with a fresh clip and chambered a round, then asked, "What the hell's going on out there?"

Hunter put grenades on the cot, and they stuffed them in whatever pockets they had available. "Sentries don't know shit. That big explosion looked like an ammo dump going up."

Minks's eyes narrowed and his voice was low. "Jap counterattack."

Hunter nodded slowly. "I think so, too. We're miles behind the lines, but I figured just in case...." He indicated the rifles and grenades. "You want me to get you one? They're just across the road."

Minks shook his head and waved the .45 caliber pistol. "I'm too weak to aim a rifle. This'll have to do. I've been keeping it under my pillow," he grinned.

Captain Bakerman burst into the tent. He looked like he'd just woken up, but his voice was clear and left little doubt that he was in charge. "Settle down, men. We're getting reports of a strong enemy counterattack. None of the information's more than hearsay right now, but something's going on. We're miles from the front lines. I doubt whatever's happening out there will reach us. I've requested more troops just in case, but until they figure out what the hell's going on, that probably won't happen."

A nearby shot rang out and they all flinched and ducked. The distinct sound of an M1 firing just outside made them scramble off their racks and lay on the floor. Some patients were too injured and simply lay as still as possible. More shots and the tent walls perforated with holes. The dim overhead light shattered, sending them into darkness. Bullets whizzed past and men grunted as bullets slammed into bodies with a distinct meaty sound.

A sentry's body fell through the tent flap and lay sprawled halfway in and halfway out. Blood soaked the canvas flap from his gaping head wound. Nearby, excited Japanese voices made them all hold their breath. They were yelling and calling to one another.

Hunter, Minks, and Mankowitz aimed their muzzles at the entrance, but Captain Bakerman put his hand out and shushed them. "Quiet," he implored. "Maybe they'll pass on by." Hunter thought it more likely they'd send a few grenades inside, but he held his fire and stayed quiet.

The soldier in the next bunk moaned. Hunter went to his side and covered his mouth and whispered in his ear, "Keep quiet, buddy. Keep quiet." He noticed fresh blood seeping from the soldier's chest. Captain Bakerman was watching him through the gloom and Hunter waved him over urgently.

Bakerman moved cautiously and Hunter pointed at the gaping wound. Bakerman ripped his tunic open and applied pressure, but it was like trying to stop a flooding river. The soldier's breathing became erratic and soon stopped altogether.

The voices outside subsided, but the sounds of running feet continued past the entrance. A Japanese soldier flung the tent flap back and nearly tripped on the dead GI blocking the entrance. His face contorted in disgust, seeing the soldier's exposed brains. He squinted into the tent, but the darkness kept him from seeing more than a few feet. He turned, yelled something, and took off running. The tent occupants breathed again, and Hunter relaxed the pressure on the trigger.

The sounds of battle continued up the valley. Sometimes it

was sporadic, other times, intense. Dawn finally broke and muted shafts of daylight streamed through the perforated tent walls and front flap.

They couldn't hear any more enemy soldiers nearby. Captain Bakerman ordered the men to push the dead bodies toward the entrance to hinder more troops from trying to enter. The grisly work was done, and the dead sentry was joined by three other unfortunate men.

Hours passed. Along the edges of the tent, they tipped over tables, cots, and anything which might deflect or stop a bullet. The sounds of battle continued. After conferring among themselves, Corporal Minks approached Captain Bakerman. "Sir, we need to get help. One grenade through the front door's gonna kill us all."

The strain in Bakerman's eyes was disconcerting. "What do you propose, Corporal?"

Minks pointed at the other two, "We'll get help. We can't sit here waiting to die. Command might not even know we're still alive out here."

Bakerman closed his eyes and nodded. "Don't let 'em see you coming outta here or they'll blow the place up."

"Yes, sir. We'll be careful." He put his hand on Bakerman's shoulder, "You saved all our asses, doc. It's time for us to save yours."

HUNTER CAREFULLY STEPPED over the dead GIs and poked his head past the tent flap. The tent was erected on a slightly higher piece of land to keep it from sinking through the tundra and into the mud. He looked due east, toward the Chichagof Valley. He couldn't quite see the sea, but the air held its scent. There were plumes of black smoke everywhere. He saw flames licking the remnants of the distant ammo dump. There was no sign of enemy soldiers, nor American soldiers.

He pushed the rest of the way past the bodies and hunched. Crouching made his leg ache, but he gritted his teeth and tried to ignore the pain. Distant machine gun fire and explosions wafted through the midday air. He moved a few feet and scanned side to side. The little bench of land was completely deserted. Without taking his eyes from the front, he waved for the others to follow.

Mankowitz and Minks stepped from the tent. Both of them winced in pain with each awkward step. Hunter thought they'd look like comically easy prey to a healthy enemy soldier. Mankowitz and Minks spread out to either side and listened. When they were sure they were alone, Hunter poked his head back inside the tent. After being outside, the inside of the tent was very dark. He whispered, "It's clear out here. No sign of Japs."

Captain Bakerman's voice came from his right and startled him. "Good. We'll stay inside, probably safer and I'm not leaving the wounded to fend for themselves."

Hunter nodded, "We'll be back with help." He closed the flap and stepped around the bodies. He joined Minks and Mankowitz. "Let's go west toward the sound of the fighting."

They moved off the raised land and used any cover they could find as they advanced. The further they moved, the closer the sound of battle became. After a half hour, they stopped and hunkered in a ditch to catch their breath. Hunter pointed. "I see someone." The others peered over the edge and saw the distant figures moving west. "I can't tell who they work for."

Mankowitz agreed, "Too risky to get their attention. Even if they're our guys, they might think we're Japs."

Minks spoke low, "Wish I had my sniper rifle. I could tell you exactly who they work for. You're right though; we can assume everyone's hostile out here."

The woodpecker sound of a nearby enemy machine gun made them duck. They expected bullets to rip into their position, but they soon realized whoever was shooting, wasn't shooting at them.

They peered back over the ledge and saw the soldiers in the distance taking cover and returning fire on the hidden MG. They were nestled on the backside of a gentle slope. It sounded like the MG was on the other side of the slope from their position.

Minks pulled himself over the ledge and Hunter grabbed his leg. "What the hell are you doing, Minks?"

"We're behind the MG. Our guys are pinned down. If we take it out, they'll know we're friendlies and they can help us out."

Hunter exchanged a glance with Mankowitz, then shrugged. Hunter said, "He's impulsive like that. It's what got him shot in the first place."

Mankowitz shook his head, "You sure know how to pick 'em, Mack."

Minks was a few feet up the slope. He looked back at them. He held his 1911 .45 but his pale, pain-filled face made him look anything but deadly. "You two coming or you gonna sit there with your thumbs up your butts?"

Mankowitz murmured, "Oh, for crying out loud."

They pulled themselves from the ditch and caught up with the corporal. Hunter put his hand on Minks's shoulder, "Let us go on ahead. You're moving like a damned wounded bull."

Minks nodded, and Hunter and Mankowitz went around him. When they reached the top of the little rise, the exchange of fire had tapered, but the occasional burst from the machine gunner pinpointed his position. He was to their right. It was difficult to know the exact range as the wind whipped and swirled, making it sound louder sometimes and more distant other times.

The pinned down GIs were even more difficult to find in the rolling tundra grasses and hills. Minks joined them at the top and gingerly went to his knees. They listened for a few more minutes. Hunter finally said, "Let's go over the top. I think he's gonna be right about there." He pointed 45 degrees to the right. "We'll be above and behind him. Shoot him in the back."

Mankowitz clutched his arm, "What if there's a rear guard?"

Minks added, "I'll watch your backs."

Hunter and Mankowitz crawled forward. Mankowitz's side ached. He could feel his stitches stretching and tugging. He wondered if it was bleeding. The machine gun opened fire, making him forget his wound momentarily.

Hunter leaned in, "Just like old times—eh buddy?"

Mankowitz nodded his agreement, but added, "The deer didn't shoot back, though."

Hunter nodded and continued crawling. They finally spotted the machine gun's position. The gunner and his assistant huddled in a foxhole beside a burnt tractor. Hunter wondered if the tractor was a victim of the morning attack or had died on a different day.

They froze and evaluated the situation for another few minutes. Hunter leaned into Mankowitz's ear. "We need to get closer. We have to make sure we kill them on the first try."

Mankowitz nodded. "Not too close or our own guys will shoot us."

Hunter gave him a curt nod, "You throw grenades, I'll do the shooting." Mankowitz nodded and they continued crawling forward. When they were thirty yards away, they stopped. The pinned down GIs fired occasionally, and bullets zinged off the metal tractor.

Mankowitz put his rifle aside and pulled two grenades from his pockets. He placed one within easy reach and clutched the other. "I—I'm gonna have to get on my knees to throw them."

Hunter had his sights on the gunner's back. He nodded, "Okay. I'll fire as soon as you throw the first one."

Mankowitz nodded and carefully pulled his knees beneath his body. His side screamed, but he swallowed the yelp trying to escape. He steadied himself and got control of his breathing, then sat up, pulled the pin, and hurled the grenade. The spoon detached and the fist-sized explosive sailed through the air and thumped into the dirt directly behind the machine gunner. The assistant turned at the sound. Hunter fired and the gunner's back erupted in geysers of blood. His body was flung forward as though pushed by an invisible hand. The grenade exploded a second later and the surprised assistant gunner disappeared behind a blanket of shrapnel, smoke, and fire.

The second grenade was already on the way. It ricocheted off the tractor and bounced back toward the machine gun nest. It exploded a second later, sending the already dead gunner's body flying over the destroyed machine gun.

Hunter was ebullient. "Damn, Mank! Nice throw. I hardly had to shoot."

Mankowitz smiled through the pain. "Thanks," he muttered, clutching his side.

Hunter pulled himself painfully to his feet and waved his arms at the distant GIs. They stood with their weapons aimed and Hunter was ready to hurl himself to the ground if they opened fire. He yelled, "We're Americans! Americans!" Mankowitz pulled himself upright and tried to wave his arms, but he felt dizzy, nauseous, and just watched with glazed, pain-filled eyes.

Four GIs sifted through the destroyed enemy machine gun nest while the other six greeted them. A sergeant from the 17th shook their hands. "That was some fine work. Damned Nips had us pinned down good. You men wounded?"

Hunter told them their story ending with, "Can you help us at the hospital?"

The sergeant who introduced himself as Sergeant Emilio Ingot, shrugged. "To say things are messed up would be a severe understatement. The Nips broke through and are spread all over the place." He shook his head sadly. "We've lost a lot of men. Some were asleep when they came through. Japs butchered 'em in their damned tents and sleeping bags. Just chucked in grenades and moved onto the next one, like they were delivering the damned mail."

Corporal Minks's jaw flexed with anger. "Dirty sons of bitches."

Sergeant Ingot nodded his agreement. "We were headed toward Engineer Hill." He pointed, "Hear that?" There was a near constant hum of battle coming from the south. "Been like that for the past hour. We were going to see if we could lend a hand but sounds like you may need us more."

Hunter nodded. "If the Japs check the tent, those wounded men won't have a chance, not the mention the doctors and orderlies."

Sergeant Ingot nodded. "You've sold me, Private. Let's go."

They spread out and moved back the way they'd come. Getting back was much quicker than their trip out and they soon spotted the top of the tent fluttering in the wind.

They approached cautiously from three sides, but there was no sign of enemy soldiers. Hunter yelled, "Captain Bakerman! You in there?"

There was a pause, then a harried voice, "Hunter? Is that you?"

"Yes, sir. We brought help."

Captain Bakerman stepped over the bodies at the tent flap and went outside. Men who could walk streamed from the tent and soon they were shaking hands with the GIs and congratulating one another.

Sergeant Ingot bellowed, "Before you get too excited, we're still in Indian country. We're behind enemy lines." To help cement his case, the wind shifted, carrying the sound of battle to them.

Captain Bakerman nodded. "What do you suggest, Sergeant?"

He scowled, "We can't move these men. Better to stay here, dig in, and prepare to defend our position."

Captain Bakerman asked, "How long till the calvary arrives?"

Sergeant Ingot shook his head, "Like I was telling the others; I've got no idea what's happening besides the fact that the Japs broke through our lines."

Captain Bakerman nodded his understanding. "We outnumber them 5 to 1. Our guys will turn 'em back soon."

Ingot scowled, "I agree. Only problem is, they'll probably push 'em straight into our position here."

Bakerman said, "We'll do whatever we can to help."

"We'll need anyone that can dig and shoot. This ain't a bad position. We've got the high ground—just need some foxholes to keep our heads down. If all goes well, the Japs won't even know we're here."

Hunter pointed to the small tent across the road, "That's where the wounded men's guns and ammo are kept. It's not much, but it'll help."

Sergeant Ingot nodded, "Let's get to work. It'll be dark in a few hours—be nice to be ready before then."

The orderlies and Ingot's men did most of the work. Hunter and Mankowitz helped, but in their weakened states, needed to take frequent breaks. Minks tried to help but passed out and had to be helped back into the tent. He slept as though someone had drugged him.

By the time the sun was setting, they'd dug foxholes around the entire small perimeter. They counted ammunition and passed it out evenly to every soldier able to fire a weapon. Ingot lamented not having a machine gun, but they had enough rifles and carbines for everyone that could wield one, and enough ammo to last through a prolonged firefight.

The sounds of intense battle continued in the south. To the relief of everyone, artillery and mortar fire entered the mix, letting them know the allies must be getting the upper hand. It was difficult to discern, but the sounds of battle seemed to get closer.

As the hours passed, Hunter struggled to keep his eyes open. Near midnight, Sergeant Ingot told the wounded to get some sleep. Most went back to their cots, but Hunter and Mankowtiz slept in their foxhole.

MANKOWITZ WAS JOLTED awake by the sound of a nearby explosion. It startled him to see it was morning. He was huddled against Hunter in the bottom of the foxhole they'd dug. They looked at one another through bleary, bloodshot eyes.

Another explosion brought them fully awake, and Mankowitz shivered, reminding him of his wound. Hunter pulled himself to the lip and peered over the side just in time to see the tail end of an explosion. He saw men in the distance cartwheeling as the 105mm shells ripped into their ranks.

Sergeant Ingot's hole was ten yards away. Hunter asked, "What's going on, Sergeant?"

Mankowitz poked his head up. Ingot kept his eyes on the morbid scene unfolding five hundred yards distant. "Japs got caught in the open. Howitzers are giving them the business."

"Are they retreating?" asked Mankowitz.

Ingot shook his head, "No. They were trying to cross from the far side to this side."

Mankowitz felt his face flush, "They're coming this way?"

Ingot nodded, "They were. Now they're just getting torn up."

Hunter chimed in, "If they're hitting them with arty, there must be friendly spotters around. Maybe they'll see us and send help."

"The ridges are full of GIs. I'm not willing to put up a sign, though. The Japs are just as liable to see it."

The artillery continued for a few more salvos, then shifted to a more urgent target. Mankowitz could see the dark smoking craters the big shells had chewed into the tundra. Dark outlines of bodies were strewn around the holes. He wondered if they had wiped the entire force out.

His hopes were dashed when he saw movement. More dots appeared and coalesced into a large ragtag group of shellshocked soldiers. They were coming directly at them.

Sergeant Ingot cursed. "Dammit! Perkins, tell the captain to get every man that can fire a weapon out here on the double." A young private sprang from his hole. "And Perkins," the soldier stopped and turned back in Ingot's direction, "That includes the good doctor."

Mankowitz whispered to Hunter, "Why the hell are they coming up here?"

Hunter shrugged, "It probably looks like a good place to fight from. They don't know we're here."

Corporal Minks shuffled his way into their foxhole and grinned. "They're gonna find out real damned quick."

Minks's face was white as a sheet, but his eyes burned with a simmering hatred. He propped an M1 rifle on the lip of the hole and sighted over it, adjusting the sights minutely. "You look like hell, Minks," stated Hunter. "Thought you couldn't hold a rifle."

Minks kept making micro-adjustments to the sight. "I don't have to. Just need to prop it up. I can still aim and pull the trigger just fine."

Mankowitz complained, "Kinda cramped in here, Corporal." Minks ignored him and Hunter and Mankowitz crammed themselves along the walls and adjusted their ammunition to accommodate Corporal Minks. "Maybe they'll stop before they get to us," murmured Mankowitz.

Minks shook his head and licked his lips. "No. They're coming all the way."

When the Japanese were still too far away to hear them, Sergeant Ingot called out, "Don't fire until I do. We don't want them to know we're here till the last second. Keep your fool heads down. If I fire—come up shooting."

Mankowitz left his rifle propped on the ledge and dropped below the edge of the hole. He wished he had his helmet. He leaned against the back wall and smelled the dirt. Intricate tiny white roots snaked through the dark soil. He realized with surprise that he'd never seen a bug. All the foxholes and trenches he'd dug and hunkered in since landing on this godforsaken island, and he'd never seen a single bug. He shook his head, wondering how his mind could focus on something so banal when death was literally marching towards him.

Minks couldn't keep from peering over the ledge occasionally, and Mankowitz wanted to punch him in the face. The son of a bitch was going to give up their position. Hunter was staring past Minks, leveling his gaze at Mankowitz. Mankowitz stared back and gave him a slight nod. He was glad his best friend was beside him. If anyone could get him through the next few minutes, it was Mack Hunter.

He had no idea how long they sat in that hole waiting for Ingot's weapon to fire, but it felt like hours. Was his mind playing tricks? He wished he had a wristwatch, but his had succumbed to the constant wetness and stopped working the first day off the boat. He didn't remember what he'd done with it.

He was pulled from his revelry by Sergeant Ingot's bellowing voice, "Open fire!" followed immediately with his barking Thompson submachine gun. For an instant Mankowitz remained frozen, unable to move. Minks fired and Hunter rose and fired a second later.

Mankowitz pushed himself up and pressed the stock into his shoulder and saw multiple targets diving for cover. They were much closer than he expected, and his first shot went wildly high. He adjusted and found a crawling target. He could only see the enemy soldier's distorted face. He was pushing himself along the ground, clutching what looked like a stick with a bayonet attached to the end. Mankowitz steadied his aim and fired. A neat hole appeared in his forehead and red mist sprayed out the back of his head.

He moved left and fired into a shape in the grass. He didn't know if the man was alive or dead. The shape shuddered with the impacts and he pulled off, searching for another target. The Japanese were all down, taking cover in the grass. It was difficult to see them without extending and exposing themselves.

Someone yelled, "Grenade out!"

Mankowitz ducked and there were multiple explosions, followed by tormented screams. An enemy screamed in broken English, "You die GI!"

Minks screamed back, "You first, Tojo!" he pulled the trigger until his clip pinged. He struggled to reload, and Mankowitz noticed. He dropped his own rifle and ripped the clip from Minks's hand and pushed it into place for him. "Thanks," Minks muttered.

Mankowitz took up his own rifle in time to see the Japanese soldiers rise as one, and with a horrifying yell, they charged. Mankowitz fired into bodies, his bullets causing catastrophic damage. Soldiers dropped and died, but there were more behind them. Bullets whacked into the tundra and he heard GIs screaming in pain and anguish.

Minks burned through another clip, but Mankowitz couldn't help him reload. Minks pulled his pistol and fired point blank into a soldier's face. His forward momentum dropped him halfway into their hole. Minks pulled him the rest of the way inside and stood on his back and continued firing.

Hunter and Mankowitz reloaded as fast as they could make their hands work. Mankowitz kept telling himself to concentrate. Ignore the crazed enemy soldiers and reload.

He finished thumbing in another eight-round clip. He didn't have time to aim. He simply pulled the trigger. His bullet smashed into the wrapped shin of an enemy soldier and cut it cleanly in half. The soldier toppled onto him and he shoved him off and away from the hole. The soldier screamed, and Mankowitz thought his head would explode from the noise.

He fired into the next man. He was charging hard and fast with his bayonet low and deadly. He fired three times, watching his bullets smash into his pelvis, then his stomach, and finally his chest. He crumpled at the edge of the foxhole and his eyes stared as his mouth gaped and blood oozed from the corners.

Hunter's M1 pinged, and Mankowitz heard him scream. He didn't have time to check on him, there were more Japanese coming fast. Minks screamed crazily and with newfound strength burst from the hole.

He fired his .45 continuously, tearing gaping holes in men's chests and faces. Mankowitz fired into two more darting enemy soldiers before his rifle pinged. He searched for another clip but couldn't find one. He ducked and felt along the bottom of the hole. His hand came away bloody from the dead soldier Minks had pulled inside.

He noticed Hunter curled in the bottom of the hole. He

had a deep gash along his hairline, and it covered his face in a thick sheet of blood. The fight went out of him. He lunged to Hunter and pulled him into his arms. Hunter's eyes were glazed. He was alive. Mankowitz rocked him, and his tears mixed with his friend's blood.

The ground shook and Mankowitz felt as though he was being bounced violently on a giant's knee. He held tightly to Hunter's quivering body, trying to protect him. The edges of the hole flexed and shed grass and dirt onto them. He thought how fitting it would be to die in the same hole he'd dug.

Finally, the shuddering stopped, and the only sound was dirt falling onto the brittle grasses. He couldn't hear it. His ears were ringing as though he lived on the inside of the old school bell at Lone Pine Elementary. He closed his eyes and rocked Hunter fiercely.

No one expected anyone in the hole to be alive. When GIs from the 17th looked inside, they'd seen an obviously dead Japanese soldier alongside two bloody GIs wrapped in a death embrace. They nearly fell over when the soldiers both startled at their touch.

They were extracted gingerly and given blankets and water. Mankowtiz looked over the battlefield. Gaping, smoking holes from danger close artillery, dotted the landscape. Dead Japanese were stacked in contorted, unnatural poses. Their mouths hung open and their eyes were staring into nothingness. GIs were carefully poking and prodding them, making sure they weren't playing possum.

Far from the dead enemy soldiers, there was a neat row of dead GIs. He counted six bodies. He couldn't take his eyes off the body on the far right. He was the only soldier not in full battle dress. He'd been a patient—it was Corporal Minks.

Captain Bakerman moved between wounded soldiers. His hands were bloody and the front of his uniform was splattered with mud. He finally got to Mankowitz and Hunter. Earlier, an orderly had checked out Hunter's head wound and decided it wasn't critical. The bleeding had stopped, and his face was crusty with his own blood.

Captain Bakerman sat down heavily beside them and ran his hand through his graying hair. He looked out over the shattered and torn bodies. "My God," he uttered. "They nearly got through. If they had, it woulda been even worse."

Mankowitz shook his head. "Minks didn't make it."

Bakerman nodded sadly, "I know. He saved a lot of good men." He looked over at Hunter who was rubbing his temples.

The little hill drew more GIs, and soon it was crawling with soldiers. Mankowitz heard his name, "Mank!"

He turned on shaky legs and saw remnants of Charlie Company filtering in. He recognized Harwick, Lance, and Numchenko striding his way. Harwick slapped his back, grinning like the Cheshire Cat. "We've been trying to get back here for hours. We kept running into Nips. Fought 'em all damned night, then we saw the arty shelling the crap out of you and feared the worst."

Mankowitz bit his lower lip. He was overwhelmed with joy to see them, but the emotions were too much, and he had to sit down. They crouched with him and greeted Hunter.

Hunter's eyes were glassy and unfocused, but he recognized the men from Mankowitz's platoon. He asked for the hundredth time, "So, what happened again?"

Hunter's wound was superficial, but whatever had hit him had given him a concussion, and for the moment, his short-term memory was only seconds long. Mankowitz didn't mind answering—he was ecstatic that his best friend was alive. "We survived, Mack. We survived."

AFTERWORD

The battle for Attu Island lasted from May 11th through May 30th, 1943. It is the only WWII battle that took place on sovereign American soil.

Although this novel is fiction, it does portray the miserable conditions and some of the actual combat situations that occurred. Most notably, Jarmin Pass and Point Able.

Colonel Yamasaki led the Japanese defense of Attu and personally led the nearly successful Banzai charge from the Chichagof Valley. It was one of the largest Banzai charges of the entire war.

The heroic stand of the 50th Engineers on Engineer Hill, actually occurred. Colonel Yamasaki's body was found among hundreds of his soldiers, still clutching his sword.

Most of my research was gleaned from a wonderfully helpful book titled, <u>The Capture of Attu: as told by the men who fought there</u> by Robert Mitchell, Sewell Tyng, and Nelson Drummond. I recommend it.

ABOUT THE AUTHOR

Chris Glatte lives in Southern Oregon with his wife and ever-present Labrador, Hoover. He has two college-aged boys who occasionally visit.

When he's not reading or writing, he's enjoying the many outdoor activities this region offers.

If you'd like to contact him, he responds to all email messages: chrisglatte@gmail.com

If you'd like to be informed of new releases, you can sign up at: chrisglatte.com

ALSO BY CHRIS GLATTE

The 164th Regiment Series

The Long Patrol

Bloody Bougainville

Bleeding the Sun

Operation Cakewalk (novella)

Tark's Ticks Series

Tark's Ticks

Tark's Ticks Valor's Ghost

Tark's Ticks Gauntlet

Tark's Ticks Valor Bound

Standalone

Across the Channel

Short Stories

Hellcat Down

Island Hop

www.ingramcontent.com/pod-product-compliance
Lightning Source LLC
Chambersburg PA
CBHW020333110726

47898CB00003B/866